Serenity Point

Christy Kyser Truitt

To Mrs. Watts
Thanks for letting us
run across the yards!
        Much love & God Bless!
                Christy

PublishAmerica
Baltimore

ISBN: 1-4241-5984-9
PUBLISHED BY PUBLISHAMERICA, LLLP
www.publishamerica.com
Baltimore

Printed in the United States of America

I dedicate this book to my husband, who gives me wings, and to my children who give me course. And to my Father who gives me eternity.

I'd like to acknowledge the girls at Envision, whose simple question of "Did you ever want to write a book?" ignited this whole journey.
And to the numerous friends that never doubted, even when I did, that this could be done.
But I especially acknowledge my wonderful family.
We should all be so lucky to have parents that save stories we wrote when we were just seven years old giving us the credibility to believe that yes, this is what you were meant to do.

Chapter 1

My mother's greatest achievement in life was her death. It provided the attention she sought with surprisingly little effort. It was the final severance between our lives first connected through the sustenance of my umbilical cord then stretched taught in subsequent years of unrequited love and mutual misunderstanding. Her final punctuation mark in life was penned on the night my father killed her therefore eliminating any chance of reconciliation.

Typing at my lady's desk in the sitting area of my bedroom with dawn slowly stretching her fingers across my black Gateway computer, I journaled my thoughts of the day with rapid clicking of the keyboard. I had finally finished the downstairs renovation although it had only been a few months and loved the way the east windows caught the morning light.

Journaling was a new habit I had acquired among several others during what family and friends have called my mid-life crisis.

My sixty-year-old father looked me in exasperation several months ago, both hands on his hips, to say, "Now, Melanie. I don't rightly know what's gotten into you. All this exercising, trashy clothes you're wearing, and now you've gone to school to learn how to rub on other people without their clothes on just like a prostitute!" referring to my enrollment at the technical college to get my massage therapy license.

He was a burly-looking weekend farmer who always reminded me of Jock Ewing from the old soap opera *Dallas*. Everyone said I looked more like Mama than him although his dirty blonde hair was now snow white. But we both sported year-round tans due to our love of the outdoors. And yet nothing in his calm, rugged demeanor could be associated with such a violent death, but his dark eyes seldom showed any life.

Well, I hope to hell it's not a mid-life crisis because that would mean I'd only live to seventy. I planned to have my mid-life crisis around fifty, still more than a decade away. Boy, that would rock their worlds if they knew the last year was only a prelude to the real crisis I planned to have later!

After completing my daily entry, I saved the screen and pulled up an electronic blank page to begin my to-do list in preparation for my date this evening. But in comparison to the pre-crisis to-do lists of last year, these bullet points seemed to be fired from a semi-automatic rifle rather than the cap gun of my previous life. But that was before I met Samuel.

After printing my list, I finished my last sip of green tea and winced as a glob of honey that inevitably doesn't dissolve slid down my throat. I slowly got up and stretched my arms, intertwining my fingers with a few knuckle pops and with a quick glance in the mirror gave myself a mental pat on my back.

"Not bad, girl," I thought to myself. My apple shape, post pregnancy body had become pear once again from various evils and pointed measures to slim my waist and shrink my thighs. If I sucked it in just right, looked at myself from the side, first thing in the morning profile, before I had anything to eat and after I emptied my bladder, you would never know I had three children, average birth weight of eight pounds, barrel their way out of my body like bronco riders out the chute in a rodeo.

And why is it that all the new exercise activities had such

romantic names like Pilates anyway? They actually sounded more like an entrée at an Italian restaurant rather than the hounds of hell they truly are. Regardless, I had finally begun to exercise because I wanted to, not because I was trying to chase out any unwanted calories from getting too comfortable on my thighs. I had met my best friend Mr. Endorphin. It was he that held my hand now during that perilous week before my period and handed me tissues during those McDonald's commercials where the little old man goes back to work. I no longer exercised because of some article I read titled, "FantASStic...Five Miles to a Smaller Butt."

I miraculously didn't consider myself as particularly unattractive anymore and happily pulled on my size eight jeans, hot pink top, high-lighted ebony hair in a twist and black flip flops to start the day. My French manicured toes peaked out of the ends like little Christmas lights on my tiny feet. There were even days I liked the way I looked, finally reconciling the borderline anorexic teenager with the ten pounds of hip of which I constantly battled.

There were more mornings than not that I actually got out of bed without making a circle around my left wrist with the pointer finger and thumb of my right hand. That may sound strange to anyone not obsessed with weight, but it is a common practice to determine whether self-recrimination will play a role in my morning. If you can feel just a little bone, then that extra roll you ate after Sunday dinner might have been okay. It was Sunday after all, even the Lord rested on Sunday.

As I walked to the kitchen to rinse out my cup, a flash of red caught the corner of my eye, and I watched a brilliant cardinal perch delicately on the bird feeder outside the bay window of the kitchen. Memories eased through my mind like warm butter on toast, and I put a hand on the mosaic granite counter to steady myself.

It was another bird on another day in what seemed like another life that took me off my straight and narrow path and chased me down that rocky slope of change. That bird may as well have lighted on my shoulder and bitten me the whole way. It was another cardinal that led me to Samuel. And Samuel led me back to life. My birth occurred thirty-six years from the day I was born.

Chapter 2

"Happy birthday to you. You're one hundred and three. I'm still in preschool, and I want my Mommy." The chorus rang out on my birthday celebration from a quartet of vocals ranging in age from thirty-six to six.

But just as I leaned over to blow out my candles, Will, our youngest and standing to my left, continued with, "My mommy's at work. She fired a jerk. She hired a monkey to do my homework," and collapsed in a fit of laughter typical of the "Will World" in which he existed.

"Now?" I asked.

"Now," they rang out, and everyone leaned over to blow out all thirty-six candles before we had to call the fire department. I'm still amazed the smoke alarm didn't go off with the plume of black that erupted from the center of the table.

I loved this about my family. We adhered to traditions as strictly as Christmas Eve on the battlefield. Everyone by silent, mutual consent laid down his weapon for at least a short time. I think I read that in *Chicken Soup for the Soul.*

Even Allie, in her ripped up jeans hung so low you could see the top of what I'm sure to be a thong, the jet black hair of both my mother and me with make-up that looked more like an outfielder for the Atlanta Braves during playoffs in the fall than the fifteen years her birth certificate claimed her to be.

Even Allie, standing to my right, showed a sense of humor

when she presented her gift from behind her back.

"Don't get too razzed, Mom," she looked at me cryptically, handing me a small manila envelope. "But I brought you something I made at school."

I looked up quizzically at my husband Rob, who only shrugged his broad shoulders as if to say, "I don't get her either."

Kit Kat, a nickname that stuck from the moment Will tried to say Katherine at eighteen months old, giggled beside Allie, in her purple gingham skirt with matching halter top and holding up her newly manicured eight-year-old hands. Kit Kat was struggling hard to decide if she was ready to be a "tween" or remain in the security of childhood for one more year.

Rob and I prayed daily it was the latter for we already had one daughter who had always matured at a rate that could swap paint with the best of NASCAR.

I bent the silver prongs on the lip of the envelope and pulled them through the hole. Grabbing the paper with two fingers, I gently slid Allie's report card free. And suddenly I found myself in the middle of one of those learning center commercials where the child gives his mom his report card for Christmas and with tears in his eyes thanks her for all her support to raise his grades. The husband and wife sandwich him in a group hug, and he probably goes on to graduate summa cum laude from Harvard. Music from the movie *Beaches* plays quietly in the background as he accepts his diploma, arms flung into the air in victory.

While the report card certainly reflected that moment— ONLY ONE C—my precious scholar merely scowled at me with a raised eyebrow wondering if there'd be a lecture for the C or tears for the B's.

"How did you get this so soon? I didn't think report cards came out until after school was out?" I asked cynically. I hated to be so wary, but we had been through so much with Allie this school year from in-school suspension for tardiness (she rides the bus for Pete's sake) and grades that have fallen faster than the birds on opening weekend of dove season in my hometown in west Alabama.

I could see the disappointment in her face and mentally kicked myself. "I'm sorry, honey. This is amazing. I'm sure you don't want me to make a big deal out of this, but I know how hard you have worked, and I am so very proud of you."

Allie was a walking contradiction—completely unsure whether to embrace her natural intellect or continue to squander in the mediocrity of her 2.0 GPA. She scored a twenty-eight on her ACT and yet barely squeaked by Algebra II last year. She'd been tested for ADD, dyslexia, ADHD and every other disorder floating across the mid-day talk shows of America today. Basically, it came down to a simple matter of her inability, or rather her culpability, to just apply herself.

"Well, miracles do happen," Rob said, looking over my shoulder. I whipped around and shot him a look that demanded he not spoil this moment for me. He shot me one back that said, "What did I do?"

Over the past sixteen years of marriage, we have held entire conversations for days without ever saying a word.

I pushed the ladder back chair away from the kitchen table and wrapped her five foot ten inches, 115-pound bones into my arms and rocked her for a moment like she was my baby again. And for a moment, she let me.

I whispered softly stroking her mid-night black hair, "I knew you could do it."

And with that, the moment passed. Allie disentangled herself from me and strode out of the room, tossing over her shoulder, "Well, don't get used to it. I only did it for your birthday. I'm going to Max's. We'll stop by the lost and found to see if we can find ya'll a clue."

Sometimes I truly felt like the greyhound at the dog track chasing the rabbit of my teenager's affections around in circles.

"Mom, hurry up so we can eat the cake. It's your favorite," Will chimed in, oblivious to Allie's departure. Truly, he had seen more of his sister's back as she left out of the house, sat at the computer, or talked on her cell phone than he had seen her face.

"What is it, Will Man? Chocolate cake with vanilla yogurt filling from TCBY?" I knew this because it was really Will's favorite, and I knew he had gone with his Dad to pick it up.

"Exactamondo. Now hurry, hurry!"

The rest of the "party" was spent opening Will's picture of the two of us, which, honestly, kind of gave me the creeps. He had yet to reach the stage where he actually fleshed out his stick figures. But at least I had progressed to black curly cues like a pick ninny on my oblong head with a particularly large, red mouth that looked like I ate road kill for lunch.

Kit Kat had written a coupon book for a spa night at "La Graham's." It was on five-by-seven pink construction paper written in colorful markers that actually bled on the paper. I adored the way she curled up the ends of her letters whenever she was writing fancy. I pulled the booklet from its severely stapled envelope, careful not to snag my fingers on the staples that didn't quite make it through the paper and read about the wonders that awaited me.

Kit Kat sat in the chair beside me, pulled my newly manicured feet onto her lap (she and I treated ourselves yesterday at the nail salon) and began popping my toes.

"Mademoiselle, eez will be my pleazuuure to relax ewe dis eeevening," she said in some crazy mixture of Spanish and French.

She was in this kick of using an entire bottle of lotion to rub my feet at night, but was I complaining? I just bought generic lotion by the boxes and kept it well within her reach. I knew this stage would soon pass, and my spa treatments would give way to IM'ing her friends on the computer.

All in all, it was a very relaxing, if somewhat disappointing birthday. I was in the middle of my foot rub when Rob barely grazed my cheek with a kiss as he ran out of the door with his fishing pole. I guess I should have expected it since my birthday fell on a Sunday, and years ago it became assumed that short of a hurricane, Rob was going to the farm to wet a hook every Sunday after church.

I take that back, he actually went during a hurricane a few years ago just to make sure his new pond was intact. We were left in the dark with sixty-five mph winds, shingles blowing off our roof and a tree dangerously close to our bedroom window. But Rob still felt comfortable in charging up the road on his white horse, I mean his Chevy Silverado, to make sure the farm survived. I remember that scene vividly.

I was standing before the front window, watching the winds bend the crepe myrtles in our front yard like gymnasts stretching before a meet. Will was on my hip, and Kit Kat had her head pressed into my rear, arms clutched around my waist. I always called that move, "Back to the Womb" although I repeatedly reminded them that it was closed for business.

"Come here, Rob. Take a look at this," I yelled at him over my shoulder. Allie, ten years old at the time, came up beside me, and we watched a raging nature decimate anything lacking six feet under roots.

Rob followed, but it was the clinking of his truck keys that got my attention over the storm.

"Where are you going?" I asked incredulously. The governor had all but requested a voluntary evacuation earlier in the day, anticipating the class-three hurricane to continue its march up the state of Alabama well into the night.

"I've got to go to the farm," he answered, not quite meeting my eyes. "You know we just dug that pond and I gotta make sure it holds up to all this water." He turned before I could respond, heading toward the garage. I quickly gave Will to Allie and ran after him—never the best thing to do when mad.

The argument that ensued was one of the more nasty ones of our marriage. We hurled insults at each other like forehands in a Wimbledon final. Always one to get the last word, I accused him of caring more for those cows and a stupid pond than he did his own family and slammed the door to the house before he could voice his reply.

I laughingly call the farm his mistress to our family and friends, but a lot of times I'm not real sure I'm joking.

Later, after settling the younger kids down for the night and getting a reassuring phone call that Allie was on her way home from Max's, I returned the phone to its charger. I kicked off my shoes, collapsed in my oversized bedroom chair and plopped my feet on the ottoman.

After reaching behind me to turn on the floor lamp, I used both hands to fluff my hair off my forehead, smelling a hint of the cocoa butter cream I slather on my elbows each night and opened my book in an attempt to finish it tonight.

I glanced at the clock that read 8:16 p.m. and thought for the millionth time in my marriage what is it a man can do on a farm in the dark with no electricity at this late an hour? And for the millionth time I shook the thought from my head—pick your battles my daddy always said—and began to read.

The words I read were not of the author Anne Rivers Siddons, but from my husband, unknowing at the time of the impact of his words on the upcoming choices in my life.

Chapter 3

I was in the tenth grade when Rob Graham literally elbowed his way into my heart. I was climbing out of my five hundred dollar, bright yellow Chevy Citation, unbelievably proud to just be driving to school instead of riding with my next-door neighbor Anna and her big sister.

I had to shut my door with my entire body because you had to lift up on the handle and push at the same time, or else the interior light would not go off, and the battery would go dead. Years later I unsuccessfully used that dying battery as ammunition against my Dad to get a new car.

As I threw my shoulder against the door and gave a quick bump with my hip, I turned to catch an elbow just above my left breast.

I don't know if there are specific nerve endings in that particular spot or maybe some untapped feminine instinct told me to play the role of the wounded victim, but tears came to my eyes as I dropped my books and wrapped my arms around my still much too flat chest.

"Holy crap! I am so sorry. I had to get my mouthpiece out of the floor board, and I didn't see you standing there," Rob stammered.

All I heard was, "Blah blah blah," because I was absolutely lost in the bluest eyes I had ever seen. I'm talking as blue as the Ninko-blue hydrangeas planted under the oak trees that now anchored our back yard. He had auburn hair that hung down in his eyes (no wonder he didn't see me), and he towered over me as I bent to pick up my books. I was so thankful I had only eaten a grapefruit for breakfast. I never found it odd that I had more knowledge about caloric intake than most dieticians, even as a teenager. With every bite, I could hear my mother's voice saying, "You know if you bite the inside of your mouth while chewing, it means you're too fat." That only happened to me once in my life, and I was nine.

I guess he was still talking while I bent down because he waved his hand in my face to say, "I said my name is Rob Graham, and I just moved this summer."

Somehow, I stood on my wobbly knees. Thank God I had the foresight to wear my new stone washed jeans and off-the-shoulder Forenza sweater, despite the ninety-degree August heat of an Alabama summer. I had saved all summer from my job as a lifeguard at the country club to buy a few essential items for school. While my Dad owned a clothing store in our town of eight thousand, he had some archaic conviction about only buying American made clothing.

So unless I wanted to wear Hang Ten or Campus my entire high school years, I had to use my own money to buy the clothes that were in style. I mean I wouldn't be caught dead without the high-top leather Reeboks they sold at the mall in Tuscaloosa.

"I'm sorry. My name is Mel—Melanie Jones, but only my dad and my friends' parents call me Melanie. Everyone else calls me Mel," I sputtered. Okay, how many times in one sentence did I have to tell the guy my name?

Oh, I had heard about Rob Graham. He grew up in an even smaller town than Sewanee, AL, spitting distance over the Mississippi line. But the buzz this summer was that he was the best running back since Bo Jackson barreled his way out of

Bessemer, and his parents wanted him to go to a more recognized high school to get a scholarship.

And Freeman High was widely known by the college recruiters because we had produced such standouts as Freddy Mason, a six-foot-two inch black wall of granite that weighed 230, but could run the forty-yard dash in 4.2 seconds. Freddy was now a commentator for ESPN 2 having blown out his knee on the opening kick-off of his sophomore season with the Atlanta Falcons in 1981.

"Well, Mel," he said, looking at me sideways, probably wondering if you can get a concussion from a shot to the chest. "I hope to see you around. I'm in Mr. Harris' home room."

Somehow I regained my composure enough to retort, "OOOh, smart boy. That means you're in tenth grade honors courses. Well, good luck keeping up with me, Mr. Grace." I whipped around and sashayed like a little girl in her first beauty pageant, rounded the corner and almost flew down the sidewalk, kicking up dust and rocks the entire way. What until Magpie heard about this!

Margaret Adams was everything I wished I could be. Her personality entered every room long before her physical presence. She had vitality; laughter and freedom surrounded her like an invisible aura that captivated her entire surroundings. She could eat every yeast roll a waiter would put before her in her life and never revisit it again. She was curvy enough to be luscious, small enough to grace the top of every pyramid. If you were far enough away from her not to be intoxicated, you may not call her beautiful. But if she was within a hundred yards of you, you either had to be her best friend or the love of her life because you knew you could reach any height clinging to her coattails.

I was lucky enough to have known Magpie since birth. Our

mothers literally delivered two floors from each other. Mrs. Adams had to have a cesarean because at conception Magpie wasn't going to be told what to do. She was so content in the womb that she was more than two weeks past her due date. And as indicative of the rest of my life, I was so accommodating as to allow myself to be delivered at one-fifty-six p.m. because the doctor had a two-thirty p.m. appointment at his tax attorney's office.

We have been inseparable since the nurses first placed us in the plastic and steel gurneys wrapped in our generic white blankets with blue and pink stripes. My cries were fits of insecurity; helpless to be so far away from the only home I'd ever known. I know now if I had not lain next to Margaret, I would have somehow scooted my way back to my mother and crawled back into her womb. I did, however, spend the next fifteen years searching for that umbilical cord. It was the only time I ever connected with my mother, both physically and emotionally.

My alter ego's cries were almost operatic. She sang soprano simply to entertain herself. She was also demanding upon her arrival, constantly keeping the nurses jumping to attention to wrap her blanket tighter, put her pacifier back into her mouth, or by golly get this nasty business out of her britches IMMEDIATELY! The nurses would later tell my daddy that I just laid there in wonder, my head turned toward Margaret perfectly content to let her be the show.

The main hall of school resembled a beehive that had just been hit with a baseball bat. The buzzing was deafening, lockers slamming, tennis shoes squeaking, girls squealing, and among the chaos, the queen bee herself, surrounded by her worker bees and drones. It was as if the pause button was hit on the VCR when you came in contact with Magpie for what you were doing was really not important anyway.

She was standing in front of a bulletin board announcing voting information for homecoming queen, club descriptions and what I'm sure caught Mag's attention, the starting line-up for Friday's football game against Meadowview.

I didn't even break stride as I gripped her arm and pulled her along as if I were swinging her up behind me on my horse and dragged her outside to the front steps facing Oak Street.

"Whoa, whoa, WHOA!" She dug her loafers into the concrete sidewalk, and I swear created sparks as she leaned back to bring me to a stop. "What is up with you, girlfriend?" She jerked her hand free and shook her wrist as if to get the blood flowing again.

Even in my excitement over Rob Graham, I couldn't help but notice how unbelievable she looked. And, as always, my new jeans and my new sweater paled in comparison to her kaki Gap shorts, knee-high angora socks and matching button-down opened just low enough to give a peak of what more than one lustful teenage boy called her jugs.

It was rumored that Joey Santori, one of the few bi-racial students in our school, told Milo Smith, "Margaret is one crazy chick. I mean, you think you're getting the red light, when really it's more like a blinking yellow that you can pass under if you look both ways and go real slow."

Whatever.

I knew for a fact he had only gotten to second base and wouldn't have gone that far, but Mags knew Mary Stuart had the hots for him. And there was no way she'd let a member of the two-name club get the jump on her.

At the time, I couldn't believe she actually went out with a guy like Joey. But, like her sister Millie said, "It's not like he's total wop. I mean his mama is white. And that's where you get most your stuff from anyway." I was not allowed to say words like that in my home, so I always felt a little guilty for Millie. Like she cared anyway. She was a senior, and we were dried crumbs stuck to the foot of the caterpillar she stepped on before getting in her new 1982 Ford Mustang this morning.

I threw my books on my right hip, hugging them like a twenty-pound toddler, and said, "You will not believe this. Even when I tell you, you won't believe this because I hardly believe it. I mean it is just inconceivable. But I'm probably just overreacting. It is not even plausible, so far reaching, even statistically improbable, that you know what? Let's just forget it. Where's your locker?"

By this time I was literally panting for air not having breathed since I whipped my long, black hair around my shoulders and left Rob Graham in what I now accept as the hope that not all girls at Freeman were as stupid as me.

"Wow, this must be really bad, since you're using all of your high-dollar words. I don't even know what you just said. But because your face is as red as my little brother's butt after he called my daddy a prick, I know there is definitely a boy involved. Spill it," she said confidently.

I giggled in spite of my torment at the thought of little Tommy in his singsong four-year-old voice calling his grizzly of a daddy a prick. Tommy was the oops of the Adams, his conception coming on the heels of a Fourth of July celebration. Big Tom felt it was a testament to his manhood that his sperm could bypass the best of birth control. Mrs. Stacey knew for a fact that it was punishment for surpassing her public limit of two glasses of Neal Holloway's firecracker punch that made her forget to take her pill.

Mags jerked my arm down and pulled me beside her on the

concrete bench placed in the breezeway connecting the main office building to ninth and tenth grade halls.

A cluster of hairspray and teased ponytails typical of the 1980s gathered in front of us, and the smell of Calvin Klein perfume surrounded us like a mushroom cloud. I heard Molly Jansen in her nasal whine say, "Oh, gawwwd. She just thinks she's all that. Mary Stuart told me that Stephanie told her that she and Mike Jacobs did it in the pool house at the country club while Reginald was unloading the liquor out back of the kitchen."

Well, Reginald was the gay, black bartender in the clubhouse that liked to gossip more than a duck liked to quack. If he knew anything about whoever it was that did Mike Jacobs in the pool house, I was rest assured that he would have told me with his wrist bent and a cluck of his tongue that always began with, "Guurl, let me tell you this."

Reginald always told me that my figure was wasted on white boys. "Guurl, you know those skinny white boys don't know nothing bout that. Yo ass is plumb wasted on dose white boys. Now us black men gotta have sumpin to hold onto." I knew Reginald was harmless, but I still wrapped a towel around my waste when I went to the bathroom in the clubhouse from then on.

Ignoring the gaggle of geese in front us, I gave a quick glance at the outdoor clock to let me know I had all of six minutes to tell Mags that I'd met the love of my life, but I was sure he thought I was the joke of his.

Once Margaret got what teenagers today call the 411, nothing would suit her except that Rob and I lived happily ever after. And she got her wish. Sort of.

Chapter 4

I saw the truck headlights flash across the opposite wall, and I knew that I still had a while before Rob came to bed. He would first bring his small igloo cooler to the butler's pantry between the kitchen and the dining room and fill it up with ice from the icemaker. Then he would go back out and transfer his fish from the live well into the iced cooler. More times than not, I would see his taillights return through the window as he would run the fish down the road to the mill houses and give away his catch. Tonight was one of those nights so I knew it would be at least another fifteen minutes or so.

My eyebrows furrowed together as I carefully unfolded the piece of paper I found stuck in my library book earlier and read his words again.

> *Dear Mel,*
>
> *I hope you find this note before I get home because you know how embarrassed I get in my sad attempts at being romantic. Nobody ever accused me of being too sentimental. Anyway, I know you have been unhappy with us and our life for quite some time, although I can't pretend to know why. I know you think I don't help enough around the house or with the kids, but every time I do, I seem to do it wrong. So, for your birthday, I thought about the thing I would like to do*

*least and figured it would be the thing you would like
to do the most.*

*So, this Friday morning, pack up the car and head
to a bed and breakfast called Serenity Point that is
located between Jacksonville and Sunset Hills,
Florida, for the weekend. I know the kids don't have
school on Friday for whatever reason, but I've got
that under control.*

*I've got a map already printed out for you from
MapQuest. It's not really that fancy a place, but I'm
sure you would rather go with about four books for
the weekend, not wear any make-up and really have
some time alone. So, I hope you are excited because I
really want to get that light back in your eyes.*

Love,

    Rob

Poor Rob, I thought to myself. Once again, he blew it.
Instead of a note that talked about all I meant to him and the
children, all the sacrifices I had made throughout the years, how
I finished my undergraduate degree with a newborn baby only
to leave my job as a fifth grade history teacher to raise our
children, he bought me this trip in order to get some so-called
light back in my eyes. Like it's my entire fault the light had gone
out when he's the one with his hand on the switch!

I mentally wrestled with myself for the next ten minutes. On
one hand, at least he's trying. I mean an entire weekend by
myself! I can't remember the last time I even went to the
bathroom by myself. And at the beach! It was only early May so
I would beat the summer crowds. Plus, I had never heard of this
place so maybe it was off the beaten path anyway.

Suddenly, I pictured myself on a long, leisurely, morning

stroll, tossing breadcrumbs to the sea gulls as the horizon blew an orange bubble that floated out of the ocean joining together land and sea in a splashing of tie-dyed colors.

But then again, what was his motive? Why couldn't he just give me a birthday present instead of a weekend of introspection? Why was it always MY responsibility to fix things? I promised he would know I fully expected him to reevaluate his priorities while I was gone. After all, I wasn't the only one running around these days like a one-armed house painter in a gale wind.

As usual, the accommodating side of me won over the indignant side of me. I once again chose my battles carefully and decided this wouldn't be one of them. To be honest, I had been thinking for some time of running away from our problems. Maybe this would be a chance to run to some answers.

Chapter 5

"Allie is at a point in her emotional state that our school has done all we can for her."

Mr. Hanks, principal of Lincoln High School, looked at us pointedly and continued, "I think she needs professional help."

I sat dumbfounded in an office I had grown quite accustomed to in the two years of Allie's downward spiral. It was the Thursday before I was to leave for my trip, and the dark shadow that always slithered across my happiness was currently seeping under the door. I knew something would prevent me from going. I only thought it would be a stomach virus or one of the kids breaking an arm. Not this balding, paunch bellied man with his soft hands and manicured fingernails folded across an immaculate desk telling me that my child was an emotional mess.

Like I needed him to tell me that!

I glanced to my right to gauge Rob's reaction, and he was methodically rubbing his chin with his fingers as if stroking an imaginary goatee.

With a sigh, I turned back to Mr. Hanks and slightly adjusted myself in the black leather chair with its nail-head trim. I wondered not for the first time how it was that a principal in the public education system of one of the lowest ranked scholastic state in the nation could afford the Manhattan leather sofa that lined the wall to the right as you walked into the office. Oil landscapes strategically graced the walls in groups of three, and the faux candle sconces flickered an electric light.

Focus, Mel, I silently admonished myself. "What happened, Mr. Hanks? Just last Sunday I got her report card, and she pulled three of her D's to B's with only one C. I thought things were improving," I asked in a slightly huffed tone. It's one thing for me to criticize my family, but mama bear comes out of the cave when threatened by outside forces.

For the next one half hour, we listened intently to what basically amounted to juvenile delinquency. Allie, Max and some other names I didn't recognize broke into the science lab and turned the flame monitor on high so that every Bunsen burner erupted like a volcano when the teacher, Mr. Spencer, flipped the switch Tuesday morning.

"At the very least, we were very lucky there was no one in class at the time, and the only damage was to the glass shields that cracked when exposed to that much heat so quickly," Mr. Hanks sternly said, emphasizing the word VERY to communicate his point. He pushed his chair back as his stomach expanded with each blow of air.

The room closed in on me, and the weight of my failure was almost crushing. I didn't even care at that time that Rob was in the room. He really shouldn't be anyway. The children were my responsibility.

I carried that burden as surely as kudzu choked the life out of a southern interstate. It was, after all, my job.

"Where is she now?" I asked. Not that I was in a real state to face my child. It was inevitable upon hearing of something I neglected in my children that I needed time to collect myself before I fell at their feet to beg their forgiveness for my inept attempt at being a full-time mother.

"She and Max were excused from homeroom and are

currently cleaning the gym bathrooms. We've already spoken to the other parents, and they've taken their children with them. All the children are suspended from school for three days, but are expected to make-up their missed assignments," he said. "We've been unable to reach Mrs. Allen."

Max Allen was a pretty good kid, or so I thought, but had a tough year with his parent's divorce. I related to his plight as an only child and unfortunately, he was the only pawn in the attempt of checkmate in his parent's marriage. Max was like the tiny bell that Colonial America would place atop the graves of their dead and tie to the fingers of the corpse below in the event a person was buried alive. A simple tug of the string would alert those above of the grave mistake below.

Unfortunately, no one ever heard Max's desperate ringing to get someone, anyone, to resurrect the security of a childhood with two parents and only one home.

It didn't surprise me they couldn't reach Lydia. She had been working two jobs ever since she came home early for lunch last June and found her husband in bed with the Presbyterian Church secretary. They were intent on finding the Lord in the most obscure places.

"Well, by God, you let her clean every one of those toilets until she can't see for the ammonia in her eyes," Rob finally piped in. "What time do you want Mel to come get her?"

After profusely apologizing and taking the business card with the name of a local psychiatrist and properly genuflecting our way out the door, we slinked away from Principal Hanks' office. I wondered just how many more times we would enjoy his company in the next two years. At least the accommodations were chic, like a page out of the Pottery Barn catalogue.

Now that's where I had seen that sofa!

"Let me tell you what I think, Mel," Rob said over the hood of my white Toyota Camry. He folded his muscular frame into the passenger seat and waited until I had secured my seat belt and started the engine to enlighten me. "This is really not as big a deal as he's making it. Sure, when you put it with all the other things she's been pulling lately, it seems bad. But I think she just got caught in a harmless prank."

As I crossed over Maple to take a right onto Broadway, I came to a rolling stop at the intersection of Broadway and Thirteenth Street. I loved this section of town, because it seemed determined to maintain its southern heritage. Although Anderson had attracted several industries in the last decade, including one major international insurance firm, downtown remained true to history.

Dogwoods and crepe myrtles dotted the median as bright yellow lantana surrounded their feet like yellow ruffles on green socks. Butterflies danced among the blooms, and life looked like the postcards sold at the Convention and Visitors Bureau that read "Visit Historic Anderson, Alabama. Where the heart beats in Dixie."

Like most small towns in the South, we hid our unwanted and unpretty away from the visiting America. We parked the elderly in a ten-story high rise two blocks over like embarrassing relatives at a family reunion. The ones that could scooted their wheel chairs out to the sidewalk with their one good foot so that the rest of us could walk by them and pretend they had each other for company. Our poor lived in what the last mayor called a planned community, which was nothing more than acres of duplexes the local banks visited at Christmas to take used toys to the gaunt and neglected children inside. The modern South could swallow its own rhetorical crap just by sprinkling a little sugar on top and eating it with its registered silver. Years later I would realize it was the only thing I could easily love even in its imperfections. It was just like me—doing the best it could do while dragging a cumbersome history behind it. It was all I ever knew.

Anderson was born from the union of two rivers when French loyalists to Gen. Napoleon Bonaparte fled France in the early nineteenth century upon his exile. These French settlers alighted from the river barges and climbed up the beautiful white bluffs shaded by sweet mimosas and honeysuckle blanketing the river to begin their settlement of olive trees and wine.

Unfortunately, the first frost annihilated the olive trees, and the grapes withered on the vines. Many left the red clay fields of Anderson for the friendlier soils of Mobile and Louisiana. But the pioneers that remained, including German slaves and lingering Choctaw Indians, settled in for slow country living, picnics in the town square and fireworks over the river.

The tremendous amount of water supply generated from the dam in the early 1900s nearly quadrupled the town's growing population, and Anderson could boast in excess of twenty thousand with a working paper mill and three lumber yards to support its community.

When Rob decided to move his construction company the ninety miles to Anderson to capitalize on the growing population, I cried like a baby being weaned from her mama's breast. I loved my hometown of Sewanee with a passion akin to one shared by identical twins. Luckily for me, Anderson shared history and tradition with our hometown so the two blended together in my mind as easily as Harry Connick Jr. and a glass of merlot.

"I don't know, Rob. Maybe I shouldn't go tomorrow." I reached down and turned the knob to send Garth Brooks to join his friends in low places and glanced to my right, forcing myself back to my immediate issue.

"Don't you dare even consider canceling your trip. I spent way too much money for you to back out now, and I'd lose my deposit. We can talk to Allie tonight. I'll ground her over the weekend, and we'll deal with the head shrinker when you get back next week," Rob said, enunciating each word with a slap on his blue-jean thighs.

I didn't have to hear his words for his tone of voice told me it was pointless to try to convince my husband that it was, indeed, a big deal, and we desperately needed to get our arms around this sooner rather than later. What would Allie think if I were to go off to the beach while she was exiled to a weekend in her bedroom?

And as predicted, our arguments fell on deaf ears. We did talk to Allie that evening, and to no surprise, we were the ones with the problems.

"Oh, you've got to give me a break, Dad," she hurled at us faster than a Jon Smoltz slider. "Big freaking deal. It's not like we killed anybody."

She sat on her white duvet cover hugging her knees and her chin resting on a zebra sham she had in her lap, looking completely bored by the entire conversation. Her hair was pulled into this wild ponytail, and she had already scrubbed her makeup off. There was actually some resemblance to the child that used to let me scratch her back until she fell asleep.

To Rob's credit, he kept his cool although the Y vein in his forehead was bulging with anger. After much protest from Allie regarding her grounding—and there was no doubt in my mind Rob meant every word for he rarely wasted words on such silly things as emotions—we walked down the stairs, passing through the dining room and the kitchen to our bedroom, flipping off lights and locking doors as we went. We were in perfect sync as we collapsed side by side on our backs onto the king-sized rice bed that we had salvaged years ago from an estate sale in Mobile.

While I didn't always agree with Rob, and, more times than not lately, I craved being alone more than I wanted to be with him, I didn't push his arm away as it reached across my stomach. Our nighttime house granted me the stillness and quiet that I daily craved, and for a moment, we listened to the steady sound of our breathing. I, too, had already dressed for bed, in my loose t-shirt and cotton athletic shorts. I can't even remember when lacy under things gave way to simple briefs, but I no longer had to dig my panties out of my rear when I slept anymore.

I heard Rob sigh in frustration as I removed his hand, got up and walked across the beige Berber carpet to the door, but to his surprise, merely locked it and turned off the fan. I pivoted slowly with a smile on my face, grasping the bottom of my t-shirt with both hands and lifting it over my head. While it had been a long time since I felt particularly sexy, one thing I knew for sure was that Rob always wanted me. I just never understood why.

And I was completely naked when I climbed onto the bed to properly thank him for my birthday present and to pretend for a short while that everything was all right in the world.

Chapter 6

I knew it wouldn't last.

I was sitting at the kitchen table drinking my second cup of Maxwell House coffee out of a cup emblazoned with Will's kindergarten self-portrait—the kind they sell for fundraisers through the school—laced with honey nut coffee mate and dreamily envisioning my weekend. I had planned to leave around seven-thirty and still had a good hour to go. Life had yet to emerge into the womb of the kitchen, but I could hear a shower in the distance with the low hum of a radio playing Faith Hill.

The table was a round oak that seated six with the middle leaf and belonged to my grandmother. It had reached its final destination into our college apartment after numerous visits to various aunts and cousins over the years. My father said he could always tell when he was at one of his relatives' homes because he recognized the furniture.

About ten minutes later, Rob came cruising by like a gust of wind that preceded a late summer day storm. He was sporting a t-shirt that had mallards cupping over a pristine lake with the words, "If It Flies, It Dies" written underneath. His wet, red hair curled over his neck like a baby's, and he smelled of soap. He grabbed his customary apple and banana and whipped by to kiss the top of my head.

"Have fun and try to relax. Don't worry about a thing here," he said.

"Where are you going?" I asked in a sharp tone. The peacefulness of the morning dropped like the bomb on Hiroshima.

"I'm meeting Scott at the Kissin B gas station, and then we're going fishing at the county lake. Hey, I put that map on your purse. I checked your tires yesterday, and your oil looks okay. You're good to go," he said, oblivious to my tone and grabbed a silver thermos from the cabinet by the refrigerator and depleted the coffee maker. There went my third cup. In Rob-world, as long as there was cash in my pocket to tip the guy who might help me change a tire, properly inflated tires to ensure that never happened and a quarter to call for help in the event my universal, always charged cellular phone somehow got struck by lightening, then he had completed his responsibility.

I knew where he was going. The who and why didn't really matter. What I didn't know was who was responsible for our two elementary age children asleep and the grounded teenager who wouldn't make an appearance at life until at least eleven.

Of course, the typical argument ensued. In Rob's predictable world, Allie was going to baby-sit the kids because he already had his day planned. Forget the fact that she was supposed to be grounded. In his mind, what better way to ground a teenager than to make her stay home with her younger brother and sister? I might have agreed with him if Allie even remotely resembled a teenager we could trust instead of someone who climbed out of her two-story window on a regular basis resulting in her father nailing it shut.

"Rob, why is it so difficult for you to understand that when a child is grounded, so are the parents? I was perfectly willing to cancel my trip to take care of this, but no, you insisted that I go and that you have it all under control," I said, barely reining in my temper. I had turned in my seat to fully face him, weight on one leg, ready to stand my ground when the argument escalated. I knew it would for this was an old dance we shared with a familiar tune.

"I do have it under control. Allie agreed to baby sit when I booked your trip."

"Did you remind her of this last night?" I asked, my voice dripping with venom. I knew it, I knew it, I knew it. I knew this was too easy. First there was Allie's episode with the science lab, and now Rob's passing the buck on his parental responsibility.

"Well, no, Mel," he said, adopting that incredibly condescending voice that I despised as much as the fact that Frito's is not actually considered a vegetable although it is a corn chip. "I thought you could wake her up before you left."

"Of course, leave it to me. Why does that not surprise me? You know, Rob, I get sick and tired of every time there is an issue with the kids, you run off to hunt or fish or play golf. Or maybe you just run off period," I yelled, the volume in my voice rising with each word.

Even I had come to hate that whiny voice I had adopted at some point in my thirties. I wasn't even sure why I was so mad except that I was suddenly very weary of being the family gift wrapper always tying up the loose ends.

"Oh, here we go. Drama central! Every time, Mel? Every single time in the fifteen years of our children's lives I run out when there is an issue?"

"Oh, come on. You know what I mean. What about every Thanksgiving? When have you ever managed to spend an entire holiday with us that didn't interfere with you killing some animal?"

His face clouded over into that look that was unrecognizable from the man I married. "Are we back to that? I ask you every time I want to take a trip if you mind, and you say no. Do I not?

Besides, you always have it so under control, what difference does it make if I'm here or not?" He yelled back, turning to face me head on.

He was right, and I knew it. I had just grown weary over the years of being the only conscience in the family. "Well, what am I supposed to say? I'm not your mama. If you can't figure out where your priorities should be, why should I do it for you?" We were squared off by that time. My feet were planted and both hands were on the island that dissected the kitchen. Rob leaned against the stove on the other side with his arms across his broad chest.

"Why is everything such a big deal to you? Cut the drama, Mel. For God's sake, I hope you can cut your poor pitiful routine long enough to try to enjoy yourself at the beach."

And with that, he turned and slammed the lid on the thermos that read *Let Graham Construction Build Your Future* and banged through the door leading to the garage, leaving me once again in the silent thunder of a room with no one left to argue.

Like I said, I knew it couldn't last. This scene was in typical rhythm of the percussion of our marriage. It would have been much easier over the years to simply record a day in our home and push the play button any time our tempers began to rise. At least we could save our breath.

I picked up the phone to call Magpie. I angrily punched in her numbers, and the poor telephone nearly flew out of my hand with each jamming button. The top knuckle of my finger actually throbbed when I was done. Why did she have to live so far away in Utah and force me to dial so many numbers just to vent my anger?

"You left yet?" She asked groggily on the first ring. Her raspy voice had the sound of someone always on the verge of laryngitis, but men found madly sexy. It always unnerved me the way she checked her caller ID and answered as if in the middle of a conversation instead of the traditional hello like the rest of the civilized world.

"I see you got my email about my birthday present. No, I haven't left yet. Naturally, I can't go anywhere without a blow up with my husband. Why should my thirty-sixth birthday be any different?" I asked in that same whiny voice.

I heard her sigh into the telephone. "Mel, get a grip. For once, don't give Rob so much control over your emotions. Take it back. Don't give him that power," she said with a sleepy sigh. I could just envision her in her Park City townhouse. It was only four-thirty in the morning there so I'm quite sure she barely rolled over in the bed and would have cut the ringer off if she hadn't seen, "Graham, Rob" on the caller ID.

She probably had on her nightshirt that read, "When you meet Mr. Right, make sure his name is not Always." I bet she had already pulled her night mask back over her eyes.

"You know, I think you had the right idea not to get married. I'd give anything to live your life at Delta. I mean, you can recreate yourself every time the plane takes off."

She sighed into the phone. "Yeah, real glam, Mel. I got in at one-thirty this morning. And after telling Captain Married Asshole for the sixth time that I had no desire to see his collection of Beatles albums, I stumbled into my bed with nobody to give a shit if I slept with Mr. Asshole or not. It's an enviable life, I'll give you that," she said in an uncharacteristically melancholy voice that was as foreign to her as the first class passengers on her last overseas flight to Tokyo. She must be tired.

I realized how selfish I was being and promised to call her after the weekend. She hung up without even saying goodbye much like she had answered without even saying hello. I guess in doing so she ensured that we would just have one long conversation for our entire lives.

Well, screw it, I thought to myself. I walked through the kitchen and climbed the hardwood staircase, glancing at the children's panel pictures on the wall to my right. Each three months of their first year of life captured in a symmetrical oval window with their expressions becoming more animated with the progressing months.

I turned left at the top of the stairs and parted the plastic, lime green beads that were nailed into the top of Allie's door. They hung loosely down her doorway clinking together like the glass bottles Miss Essie used to hang in her trees outside her clapboard house to ward off the haints. Miss Essie was my other best friend growing up despite the seventy-year difference in our ages.

I walked the few steps to Allie's bed, carefully avoiding the cordless telephone, remote control to the TV and other items of clothing that compiled the landfill of Allie's room. It had a slight smell of dirty socks, bubblegum lip-gloss and antiseptic skin cleaner.

"Allie, I'm about to leave. I wanted to make sure you knew that Dad had gone fishing, and you were in charge of KitKat and Will," I said softly, brushing her hair out of her eyes so I could see some life. I was desperate for someone to hold me and at least feel some sadness that I was leaving.

Nothing.

"Allie," I said a little louder, giving her a shake.

"Jesus, Mom," she barked, her face looking as if she was told she was attending a Wayne Newton concert for her sixteenth birthday. She rolled back over and pulled the sheet over her head.

"I've got to go, Allie, and I need to know if you heard what

I said. And don't bring Jesus into this," I couldn't help adding.

"I heard you. Have fun. Don't mind me sitting here all by myself this weekend with the little monsters. You just enjoy your time at the beach while I didn't even go to the beach last year. Forget that Sally went twice, and even Max went with his Dad. Just have fun," she mumbled. I could see her mouth moving beneath her white cotton sheet like Egyptian royalty carefully wrapped for preservation.

I knew it wasn't the time to remind her that Max's trip with his Dad was guilt time because he actually missed the boy's birthday. With a sigh, I kissed her cheek, or rather the sheet, and turned to go. I stepped across the hall to Will's room, but his snoring assured me he was another hour away from life. I swear that boy could raise the roof off a barn full of chickens with his snores.

Kit Kat was sitting in her bed playing with her American Girl doll named, appropriately, Kit, when I walked by her room.

"Hey, sweet cakes. What's up?"

"Not much, Mom. What's up with you?"

"I guess I'm about to leave. Dad has gone fishing, and Allie is in charge until he gets back. It should be around suppertime," I added optimistically, leaning on her doorframe.

"Yeah, right. Like that ever happens," she said knowingly. My middle child was wise beyond her years.

Magpie used to hold her three fingers up securing her pinky behind her thumb. She'd pull the pointer finger down to say that was Timmy. She'd pull her third finger down to say that was her older sister Millie. That left what we called her bird finger standing proud.

"That's me," she'd say. "I'm the one that tells the rest of them to go to hell." Did KitKat feel that way?

"Well, anyway. I hope you have a great weekend, and I will call you when I get there. Try to stay out of Allie's way because she's supposed to be grounded," I said, walking to her white wicker bed and leaning on one knee to fluff her overstuffed, purple fuzzy pillow.

I placed both hands on her cheeks, squeezed them together in little dough mounds and kissed her on her puckered lips. I then pushed myself off the bed with one hand and left the room before I changed my mind about the whole thing.

"Allie's always grounded, Mom. Have fun and read lots of books. I'll take care of Will," she called after me.

I carefully closed the front door and pulled again to ensure it was locked. I could hear the hum of Mr. Watson's push lawn mower grow louder as he marched toward me next door. The heat blasted around me like I had opened the oven door after pre-heating, and I dreaded the summer lurking around the corner. I stuck my hand up in a wave that suggested I was glad that was he and not I. The smell of fresh cut grass still wet from the dew stung my nose. I walked purposefully to my car, holding my cornflower blue Samsonite suitcase in my right hand, my purse and keys in my left.

The suitcase had been a high school graduation gift to my mother from her parents, and one of the few things I had kept when she died twenty-one years ago. I had never used it, but dusted it off for nostalgia reasons to hopefully inspire whatever self-awareness I was intended to discover this weekend.

As I loaded the trunk of my Camry with my sparse belongings, I looked up at the house I had shared with my vagabond family for the past twelve years.

The sun was still traveling its way up the older white two-story Victorian with black shutters on the two bottom windows and the three upper windows. Shadows blanketed the west side as light slowly crawled across the wrap-around porch like a mother pulling the blankets off a sleeping child.

"Goodbye my flowers," I said out loud to no one in

particular, bidding farewell to my four hanging baskets of red chrysanthemums flanking the front stoop because I knew they would be dead before my return. Will's skateboard and KitKat's roller blades were tossed by the front box-hedge just off the stamped concrete walk waiting for the next rain to rust them into oblivion.

My eyes followed the walk to tread easily around the wrap-around porch, moving among the wicker rockers and white wrought iron antique table holding a bucket of impatiens with variegated ivy trailing down its side. The kids and I had painted the wood floor of the porch a peony blue last summer and the ceiling a Kennebunk Port green to give it an inverted earthy look. Three white fans wobbled around, forcing the stagnant hot air into movement.

Our backyard was filled with oak and maple trees with blankets of hosta at their feet. Rob cursed the landscape every time he cut the grass, but I was proud of our picture perfect home. Looking outside in, it was easy to assume everything was as perfect there as well.

All in all, we had about two acres, unheard of in our county, which was deemed the fastest growing in the state due to our highly recognized public school system. Maybe that's how Mr. Hanks' got his fancy office.

I slid into my seat, reassured by Rob that my air balance and oil gauge were properly in order. I swear the man will take his air pressure tool to the funeral home to check the tires on my hearse before it leaves for the cemetery. I placed my cell phone in the cup holder to my right, turned on the ignition and carefully backed out of the driveway onto the road that would take me away from my security and my history, unknowing at the time it was taking me to my destiny.

Chapter 7

"Miss Essie, did you always love your mama?" I looked up from the front stoop of her wooden, frame house, with my right hand over my eyes in a salute to the noonday sun.

"Lawd, chile, what a question to come ou cha mout of sech a li'l chile," she said, rocking in her front porch chair, making a sort of popping sound as it went back and forth over the uneven wood.

I was only seven at the time, which would make Miss Essie a "shade unner seventy, Ah's reckon" as she would say.

"Miz Melanie, Ah's reckon we all don love our ma's like we shud," and that was all she said. We had been best friends for about a year now, and she knew to keep quiet long enough for me to spill my worries.

"Why does my mama make me wear dresses all the time? They're always too tight around my stomach, and she screams at me when I stretch them out to where I'm comfortable. I don't like these shoes. They're too shiny, and I have to spit shine them before I go home from your house every day, or else I will get in trouble because your road ain't paved, and she'll know where I've been," I said as a roll of thunder mumbled in the distance. I loved being able to say words like "ain't" at Miss Essie's house. Such incorrect grammar would earn me a bite of soap back home.

I wasn't allowed to leave the woods behind our house, but

41

ever since I found the dirt road at the outer edge of the pine trees, I ran up and down that road for miles and days. It was just my secret. Even Margaret didn't know anything about it. Especially about Miss Essie. It was my only act of defiance in an otherwise orderly childhood.

I grew up in the 70s, the decade where advanced southerners liked to pat themselves on the back for living within walking distance of the coloreds. Heck, we even changed the name of the high school to honor a former slave. We sat beside them at the lunch counter of Walt's Drug Store. Coloreds no longer had to walk in protest to drink out of the same water fountain, and the "Blacks Only" bathroom at City Hall was now a janitorial closet.

Yessuh, Sewanee, Alabama, was quite the progressive city.

But to visit an old Cajun woman, born outside New Orleans to the illegitimate daughter of a mulatto, not just on her front porch, but in her home at her kitchen table? Well, that just ain't something to brag about while drinking your red kool aide out of paper cups in Miss Frannie Baker's second grade vacation Bible school class.

"Miz Melanie, iz bees lak dis. Lots o mamas laks to raiz deys chirren jes to spite deys own mamas. Ah reckon yo ma jes wants you ta have what maybe she din't when she was a chile. Whacha thank?" she asked, placing both hands on the arms of her chair and slowly pushing up. I loved watching the back of her arm flap with the effort. She had a burned place on her upper arm where she had leaned against an oven door. It looked to me like a slice of melted cheese. I always wanted to touch it, but never did.

"Come on, chile," She said, not waiting for me to answer. "Let's go get some lemonade so's you can getcha home fore dis rain."

Lemonade with Miss Essie was the soothing balm on the burns of my childhood. It followed many a discussion on that front porch. Like the time Mama burned my hair trying to give me an Olgivie Home Permanent for the Sixth Grade Beauty Pageant that I didn't want to be in the first place. Or the time she whipped me with a brush for using her red fingernail polish to write my name on my new bike. Or even when she would hit on my teachers during conferences while wearing strapless tops, daisy duke shorts and high heel shoes. Or the worst was the confusing and rare times when she would unknowingly scratch my arm while reading a magazine if I were silent enough to scoot in beside her. Miss Essie would just "tsk" her tongue and go pour me some lemonade.

I knew it was the upcoming rain clouds that reminded me of Miss Essie as I made my way down I70 at a slow clip. Some of my favorite memories were sitting on her front porch listening to the rain splatter against the tin roof, making music with the occasional clap of thunder and thumping of the wind through the magnolia trees that littered her small yard.

I never did tell anyone about Miss Essie. I guess about high school, I quit caring what anyone would have thought, but yet still protected my time with her. I think subconsciously I knew how much I needed her wisdom and maternal support; I certainly wasn't getting it from my own mother. She was too busy burning stickpins with matches in order to puncture my pre-teen acne and then burn the sores with alcohol just in case it dared to return.

What drew me initially to Miss Essie's home was a sign posted on a stake in her front yard, written in black magic marker on the back of the front flap of a Rite Cola box, that said:

Rabbits Fer Sale:
Pets or
Meat

She was sitting as she always was, in her front rocker, wearing a simple cotton dress, sort of a tea color probably faded through the years with purple violets. It was haphazardly buttoned, one side hanging longer than the other and knee high stockings rolled down like socks over her coffee-colored orthopedic shoes.

She always had on a stocking cap, no matter the temperature and from that day forward greeted me with, "Good morning, chile. Where ya at?" gently stroking the rabbit she would hold in her lap.

I asked her one time how she could love the rabbits so much if she was willing to kill them for meat.

"Lawd, chile," I didn't remember a sentence she uttered without those words first. "Gawd done put dees here rabbits in my care. Soms job is to give love. Soms job is to give life. T'aint for me to know. Just the Lawd's."

She was always matter of fact about life, and that's what I loved most about her. Tell it to you straight, she would, and never mince any words. It took me some time to understand her Cajun accent, but she had lived long enough in Alabama— nearly twenty years—to soften its twang and separate her words enough to grab a line here and there. I met her daughter when Miss Essie died during my junior year of college. I never did know what happened to her husband. I returned with her to the small house following the three-hour funeral to help her pack up Miss Essie's things. It only took two boxes to complete Miss Essie's life. My memories, however, would fill up a lifetime.

The six-hour drive to Serenity Point literally flew by, as it was mostly interstate. I looked at the map I had placed on the console and reassured myself I had not missed my exit.

Rob had handwritten notes along the margins:

Turn left when you get off Exit 134. It gets tricky here. Set your odometer and go 2.1 miles. You'll take a right onto Highway 231 west. There should be an Exxon station there. Stay straight for another 15 minutes or so then look for a Baptist church. The first dirt road to your left is the drive to Serenity Point. There's no sign so be alert!

Again, typical Rob. He probably got on a GPS web site to get so specific directions. I might silently wallow in my anger towards him the entire way on a trip, but I would arrive on time with no automotive incidents.

Twenty minutes later, right according to schedule, two fingers of a dirt road beckoned me to turn left. The gentle spring rain that had preceded my arrival had patted down the earth with its gentle touch. I wound my way down through the giant oak trees with the traditional Spanish moss dripping from their branches, as you would expect on the northeast coast of Florida.

The dirt road folded into cobblestone, and I slowed the Camry to enjoy the uneven road. In the historic district of Anderson, there were several streets that were still laid with the brick original to its 1829 origins. There, as I did now, I would drive slowly and imagine myself in a horse drawn carriage, making my afternoon calls. I probably wouldn't be a Scarlet— more like a Sue Ellen, destined to sit in jealous agony in the shadows of her glamorous younger sister. Margaret would have been my Scarlet. If it weren't for my love of air conditioning and instant coffee, I would swear I was reborn this century following my turn as a nineteenth century southern belle.

The final bend curved around a cluster of native dogwood trees and one gigantic willow whose branches swayed in the ocean breeze like the long arms of a musician gently stroking a harp. I passed a hand-painted wooden sign that read, "What's Ya Hurry?" and pulled around the circular drive fronting the impressive two-story beauty showing a hint of the ocean just over her right shoulder.

I could smell the fragrant blend of jasmine and honeysuckle when I opened my car door and slowly stretched my way out, stiff from the long ride. I rounded the car to the trunk, but before I had time to set my suitcase on the ground, an older man, probably about my Dad's age, suddenly swung open the front door and skipped down the steps like a child playing jump rope. He looked like an elf with a shock of white hair escaping from a red baseball hat that read, "I'm spending my children's inheritance."

"You must be Melanie Graham," he sang out. "We weren't quite expecting you this early, but so glad you're here safely. Here, let me get your suitcase. Can't be having a lady toting her own suitcase, now can I?"

Before I could reply, he flitted around me and took the suitcase out of my hand.

"Now, calm down, Nathan. Let Ms. Melanie breathe. He still gets so excited when new guests arrive," a voice spoke from behind a swollen hanging basket overrun with purple verbena, sunflowers and caladiums, an odd mixture that suited perfectly. I could just make out her bare feet standing on the tips of her toes as her arm stretched up to tip over the green watering can into the flowers.

Setting the can on the front step and wiping her hands on her ample hips snug in her navy capris pants, she pushed her short, silver hair behind her ears. She made a "tsking" sound with her tongue as she walked toward me with a smile that could make the devil's choir sing Halleluiah.

"Ain't she pretty?" Nathan asked with a grin. "Just look at those brown eyes, looks like a tootsie roll pop. And she's even older than me. I tell you what. If I had a mule with a fanny like hers, I'd plow all day long!" He bounded up the steps like my suitcase was a school lunchbox and into the house before I even spoke a word. I couldn't help but grin.

"He's a harmless old coot. Retired five years ago from BellSouth, and you would have thought he was one of the slaves that rode the Underground Railroad to freedom. Hi, I'm Mary Beth Giles, and you have had your first experience with my husband Nathan. Just wait until he pulls out his fiddle tonight. Quite the show!" She chuckled.

Mary Beth spoke in that wonderful dialect indigenous to the true south. Not the bastardized version of redneck origins thrown around today, but beautifully drawn out syllables. Almost like a child who stretches her gum from her mouth as far as it can go until it breaks.

As we walked into the house, I learned that she and Nathan had come to Serenity Point for their twenty-fifth wedding anniversary and fell in love with the area. Twelve years later, they bought the home and adjoining five acres including a mile of beachfront property when the owners, an elderly couple named Martha and Eugene Hughes, decided to live with their daughter in Virginia.

"Precious couple. Just the best," Mary Beth said, opening the screen door with a gentle hand on my back, guiding me into the front hall. "But after Ms. Martha broke her hip, they just couldn't keep up the place anymore. We had been back many times and kept in close touch with the Hughes.

"It was never a secret that we wanted to buy the place. Well, the Lord sure opens windows when he closes doors, yes he does," she recalled, shaking her head as she told me about the early retirement package that BellSouth had issued Nathan just days before the phone call came from the Hughes.

While she reminisced, I took the opportunity to look around and began by looking up. A massive six-arm Victorian chandelier dripping with crystal tear drops twisting into rose pattern shades crowned the dome ceiling in the front foyer while triple crown molding framed the twenty-some-odd foot walls. I just caught the backside of Nathan as he bounced up the spiral cypress staircase with a Persian rug running up behind him. Did anyone wear shoes around this place?

The oak paneled foyer reflected the accent light of the chandelier like satin, and period portraits with brass candle sconces covered the halls. A calico wove its way around my bare legs and strode haughtily into the sitting area to my immediate right. He lighted onto one of the antique love seats the color of tomato soup in front of a working fireplace, sauntered around in a circle twice and then collapsed into a brown, white and black ball of fur.

I could hear dishes clattering down the hallway, and a door opened just beyond the staircase to reveal a dining room big enough to accommodate my entire one-hundred-plus members of the senior class at Freeman's High School.

"As I was saying," Mary Beth said, drawing me back into the conversation. "We normally don't have check-in until three p.m., and we've already served lunch. Mavis is just now drawing up your room. I've put you in the Magnolia suite. We just painted in there about a month ago.

"Let me get you some cheese and crackers and a mimosa, and you just relax on the porch. We'll get you in within the hour. You do take champagne with your orange juice, don't you?" She asked, tipping her head to the side. As round as she was, everything about Mary Beth was dainty, even her tiny ears poking out from under her eyeglass chain. She and Nathan were like Keebler elves working hard to produce those wonderful fudge striped cookies that I would sneak into my childhood bedroom after dinner.

"Is there any other way?" I asked, not entirely joking. I grew up with a mother whose morning began with coffee laced with bourbon. Her goodnight kisses reeked of cigarettes and red wine.

Mary Beth handed me a brochure about the history of the property, and luckily I had a paperback in my purse, which I had managed to wrestle from Nathan's generous welcome. It was my latest self-help book about finding your inner purpose. I believe that made it number twelve on my list, but I had long stopped counting. She nudged me out the front door again with promises of crackers and champagne, and the screen door squealed in protest to so much activity.

I found a white wooden swing to the right of the front door made comfortable with giant plaid pillows in brilliant greens, yellows and fucias and fringed in black. The black wicker furniture was adorned in similar patterns, and I made a mental note to ask Mary Beth if she recovered her furniture herself.

With a relaxing sigh, I nestled myself into the downy pillows, unwinding enough to take off my sandals and prop my feet up on the swing. I opened the brochure that read, "What's Ya Hurry?" and learned the sweet and tragic history of Serenity Point.

Serenity Point was originally built in the early 1800's by Dr.

Beaford Hughes, a veterinarian in nearby Tallahassee as a weekend retreat for his family. Several northern industrialists, one of whom deeded the original two hundred acres to Dr. Hughes, had developed the community of Sunset Hills.

The brochure explained that as Dr. Hughes made his daily rounds to the outlying farming community of Sunset Hills, a man ran up to his wagon and grabbed his horses by the reins. It seemed as though the man's son had been on the wrong end of a rattlesnake, and the quick-thinking doctor took out his pocketknife and carved an X into the snakebite. The blood flowed freely from the wound, taking with it the poisonous venom. In appreciation for saving his son's life, the man deeded the property to Dr. Hughes.

The massive house was originally three stories, sixteen thousand square feet with all the amenities of the day. Three floor-to-ceiling fireplaces graced each level, and the three Hughes children ran freely up and down the spiraling staircase, occasionally sliding down the cypress railing when no one was watching. Even Dr. Hughes' mother would grace the front porch when she visited from New York, calling after the children, "What's ya hurry?"

Until, tragically, Mrs. Hughes died after a long battle with malaria. Feeling enormous guilt for not saving his wife, Dr. Hughes ordered a crew to destroy the third floor of the house for that was where her sickroom lay, as she loved to open the eastern windows to hear the roar of the ocean as it crashed onto the shore. The roof was lowered to accommodate the two stories that remained today.

A Hughes had always lived in Serenity Point, even when it became a bed and breakfast in the early 1930s. Sadly, Martha and Eugene, great grandson of Dr. Beaford Hughes, had no sons to take over the home, and their daughter could not—or would not I thought to myself—leave her successful child psychiatry practice in Virginia. So, the property was sold to the Giles' whose long-time love affair with the home ensured its continued tender care.

I must have dozed off in my reading because when I opened my eyes, I saw a tall glass of orange juice on a bright orange platter filled with a bushel of grapes, saltines and a block of cheddar cheese sitting on the rectangular table in front of me. In answer to my growling stomach that had no nourishment since I stormed out of the house at eight this morning, I hungrily wolfed down several cheese crackers and chased it with my spiked orange juice.

I don't know what it is about mimosas, but I always feel a little hazy after the first glass. Not seeing any sign of the Giles', I decided to weave around the side porch to the back of the house and take a look at the beach.

Suddenly, a color redder than a virgin's face on her honeymoon caught my attention as I watched a cardinal sail onto the black light fixture by the front door.

He thrust out his black chest proudly, and his masked face gave me a smirk. Catch me if you can, he seemed to say, and took off around the house.

"Okay," I thought to myself. "Why not?"

I followed down the front steps and made my way past the concrete birdbath and shepherd hooks that held the wind chimes in the side yard. I scanned the holly bushes and intertwining honeysuckle vines for my new friend with my right hand shading my eyes; I suddenly noticed that I wasn't alone.

A man at least six foot three inches in bare feet with wind-tossed blonde hair wearing a blue pin-striped shirt with the sleeves rolled up, untucked over cacky shorts and no shoes, was walking up from the beach, through the pampas grass. His left hand was in his pocket, and his right one carried a novel. He looked like he stepped off a Land's End magazine cover. He glanced my way and squinting his eyes against the sun said, "You must be Melanie. I've been waiting for you. I'm Samuel."

Chapter 8

The day ran away from me as it usually does when I'm forced to read a new book, or in this case, an old book that I was reading in a new light with an older mind. It was *The Old Man and the Sea* by Ernest Hemingway, one of the many required readings of my childhood that I merely glanced through on my way to purchasing the Cliff Notes version. Ironically, I don't remember the Cliff Notes being less pages than the book. I realize now that I could have read the actual book much faster. I can remember my mama's protests to this day.

"Now, Samuel, how are you ever going to learn anything if you don't put in more effort?" She would look at me, in her perfectly pressed silk suit with real oyster pearls smiling around her neck.

"Mama, I don't understand the big deal. I make straight A's, perfect in conduct, letter in basketball. What is there to complain about? At least I'm not like Stan who you guys throw a party for if he makes a C."

"You leave your older brother out of this." She pronounced her er's like ah's so that it sounded more like brothah. "At least Stan can tell me a month from now what he learned today because he has to work so hard for it. Just because it comes so easily for you, don't you take it for granted so much. You've got two more years of high school to go, so you better slow down and actually learn something."

Martha Louise Webster Patterson was and remains today the quintessential southern woman. A raging intellect trapped in a society that puts more value in the jewelry around her neck than the power in her mind. So my mother and those like her are forced to merely carry the genes of their genius and pass them along to the more applicable minds of their sons and subsequent grandsons. And it is only the southern male offspring that ever truly know in his heart the origin of his greatness.

So, in honor of my mother, I chose this great, albeit short novel that surprisingly showed a remarkable parallelism to my own life. I could readily see myself as Santiago, rowing aimlessly out to sea, searching day in and day out for that elusive big fish. Although with me, I was searching aimlessly for a purpose to live again. If I found it, would I wrestle as determinedly as he to bring it to shore? Or would I give up at the first shark attack and once again allow life to swallow up my prize?

I had my own demons to conquer and chose this week to ambush the enemy. I had lain docile for the past year, allowing my misery and self-contempt to shroud me in a cloak of anonymity. Maybe that is why I chose to re-chart my career from ambitious commercial real estate attorney to the less grandeur defense of the defenseless. I had championed the downtrodden and abused for the past year, struggling to provide a way out for those in the final seconds of the fourth period of life with no time-outs. And the successes came, along with a great sense of satisfaction. And yet that satisfaction never blended over into my personal life. I came to Serenity Point to figure out how to find my way back.

It was the bed and breakfast I kept promising my wife Sarah we would visit as soon as this land deal closed, as soon as I received the rent rolls on this apartment complex, as soon as we cleared the multiple liens on this million dollar office complex so we could roll the construction loan into more long-term commitments.

Sarah was unbelievably understanding of my work in the early years of our marriage. She married me the last year of law school because she said she would never see me again once I hit the big time so she figured she'd tie me down then. Little did she know by that time I was just as determined to have her as my wife and part of my motivation to give her the kind of life she never had growing up. I was the typical silver spooner while she worked from the time she was thirteen years old in order to pay for her schoolbooks.

She was a waitress at the coffee shop where she poured me caffeine while I poured over law books. She instinctively knew when I needed a break and was always there to give me a joke to keep me going.

"Hey, did you hear about the plane crash that killed those Brazilian people?" She asked me on a particularly stormy night when I was struggling to stay awake while reading *Principles of Property Law, 2ⁿᵈ Edition.*

"No, pretty little waitress that makes me laugh, what happened?" We had known each other for several months, but I had yet to work up the nerve to ask her out.

"I didn't catch the whole news report. Gosh, I don't know how many a brazillian is, but it sure sounds like a lot." And she would saunter off in her cheesy diner uniform leaving me the few minutes it would take to catch up with her punch lines. I asked her out the next night, and we were together ever since.

That is until she died last year.

That's what brought me to Serenity Point. I arrived on Wednesday, hoping to put some distance between my parents and me. Oh, their intentions were good; they knew it was the first anniversary of Sarah's death. But I'm like the crystal glass that had been splintered, but yet still maintained its form. But all it would take is one touch to shatter into tiny pieces. I'd rather be alone with Sarah, get direction from her on what I'm supposed to do now. And to ask her forgiveness for taking for granted the life we had together thinking it would last forever.

The last couple of days had been kind of slow. The biggest excitement had been the Sunset Group from a church in Georgia. I had to admit to crushing pretty hard on one in particular, Mrs. Marion Beecham, who used to act on Broadway. I saw her standing on the side porch one morning with one foot on the railing and leaning over sideways to stretch one arm down her leg. I could tell through her black spandex leggings that she still had thighs that could crush a walnut, and I fell in love with her that instant. She was at least seventy years old.

It was nice to be the youngest guest at Serenity Point, and I certainly enjoyed being fussed over. Each dinner, I would gallantly hold out the ladies' chairs while kissing the proffered hands of more than a few. The old fogies liked me as much because I would listen intently while they regaled the tales of their youths. Hunting trips in which ten-point bucks were felled instantly with one shot of the bow. Women that would swoon at a single puff of the cigar. Justice that was meted out by the shake of a hand and an intimidating stare rather than the blood of a knife.

Friday rolled around, and Hemingway and I made our way to the beach. It seemed fitting to lose myself in a novel about the sea while the subject matter itself pounded against the shore to get my attention. About mid-afternoon, I realized I had not eaten since breakfast, so I decided to head back to the kitchen.

The day wasn't as blistering hot as its predecessors. There was a hint of a coming rain. The air was a little soupy, condensation thickening its feel. The beach at Serenity Point was private so there weren't any tourists around, and the only sounds were the waves and my own memories of Sarah rolling through my mind. But I had made it through yesterday. And I would figure out how to get through today. I knew I wasn't promised tomorrow.

As I walked through the pampas grass, which formed the natural path leading from the beach, I sensed someone coming around the house. It was then I noticed her.

She had the blackest hair I'd ever seen. Blacker than the backs of my eyes when sleep alluded me. She was a great deal shorter than I, which is not unusual given my height. She was tan even by Florida standards, which gave her an exotic feel when blended with her dark hair that fell loosely to her shoulders. And, being the male that I am, I admired the graceful turn of her neck and noticed she moved her head as if unsure of herself, her arms wrapped around her waist as if to protect herself from something. Her posture intrigued me as I had seen it often in the women I represented. They would unknowingly drop their shoulders and walk with their heads down in an effort not to call attention to themselves. I found it curious to see this in what I assumed was our expected guest. I knew we were expecting a female guest today, traveling alone, but that was all I knew about her.

She stopped to pick up a piece of paper that had blown in from the beach and put it in the pocket of her black walking shorts. Then she straightened as if looking for something and turned to me as if I was what she was looking for.

I cleared my throat a little, surprised at my unusual sense of shyness and approached her with what I hoped to be an unthreatening manner. I offered her my left hand as I still held my book in my right and introduced myself, grateful to have someone within my generation to at least talk with at the dinner table. Maybe the weekend would be more endurable after all.

Chapter 9

As his right hand was full, I took his offered left hand in mine while hearing my father's voice shout, "Stranger alert! Stranger alert!" in my head.

But I felt his wedding band pressed against my palm and felt comfort in knowing his wife was probably dragging behind him with all the beach belongings while sunburned toddlers cried in worn-out misery. Typical, I thought.

"You were waiting for me? Well, where's the marching band?" I asked in an uncharacteristically flirty voice. I could have cared less that my hair had that sticky wild look as if I had just combed it after finger painting with glue. I wasn't here to impress anyone. I didn't think twice about the mascara smeared under my eyes or the fact my mother would get the belt if she saw me without lipstick. Okay, maybe I did think twice because I'm sure the distant thunder was my mother either stomping her foot on the ceiling of heaven or knocking on the roof while glistening in a much hotter climate.

I introduced myself. "Are you staying here?" I continued, turning towards the house while glancing over my shoulder for the harried wife and small children. I wondered what was keeping her.

"I'm sorry. I guess that sounded kind of forward. It's just that I've been here a couple of days now, and all I've had for company are the ten members of Sunset Group from Holy

Trinity Presbyterian Church in Gainesville, GA, average age eight-two, and Moses the cat," he lamented, hanging his head in mock sadness. "Ms. Mary Beth told me to hang on that the young folk would arrive this weekend. And here you are! So, let me try again. I'm Samuel Patterson, and I'm sure glad you're here to save me from the geriatric Holy Roller Tour of Florida."

"Yes, here I am," I said gamely. I wasn't real sure where this was going. But strangely, I felt at ease with him as we walked towards the front of the house. It was generic conversation, mostly about the beautiful weather the past week with a few passing thunderstorms. But Samuel was so not threatening; we were immediately like old friends at a high school reunion. He said he was staying in the Pine room, which was down the hall from mine.

"I guess I'd better move my car," I said lightly, absently fussing with my hair while retrieving my keys from my purse.

"Not a bad idea. I found out the hard way ol' Moses likes to walk up and down your windows and leave his dusty footprints in his wake," he said with that same lopsided grin, and I noticed for the first time a slight dimple in his right cheek. He had that preppy, fraternity boy look. I noticed his skin was freckled, and his shorts hung off a slender waist. His collarbone protruded through his shirt as though he had experienced a rapid weight loss, maybe a recent illness.

He wasn't unattractive, but I normally gravitated toward the meatier build of football jocks. At least that's how I would describe Rob. He played football, basketball and baseball and even worked summers tending the public ball fields for the city. He had a perpetual farmer's tan, and this guy looked like the underbelly of an albino deer. Still, he had an expressive face whose eyebrows moved rapidly with his mouth an interpreter for the deaf.

"I'll save you a spot at dinner," he said, giving a mock salute and half-turning to jog towards the house.

A feeling of familiarity and almost serendipity rushed over me as I drove around a grove of trees to the guest parking area. Normally, I am very nervous in new situations, biting my fingernails to a nub and chewing my cuticles raw. It had yet to occur to me to be so at Serenity Point. It was like meeting the cousin of your best friend while on summer vacation. Shared intimacies bond you at the first hello.

I saw Mary Beth on the porch beckoning me inside as I walked up the gravel drive.

"We got you all fixed up. This is Mavis," she said with her hand on the arm of a rotund, elderly black woman. "Mavis worked for Martha and Eugene for years, and we were so lucky she decided to stay with us. Just don't know what we'd have done, no we don't."

I followed Mavis up the winding staircase, pausing every couple of steps to admire the antique iron works along the wall and to allow her to catch her breath. She reminded me of the long forgotten Hawaiian Queens that ruled the islands before eager Christians rowed ashore to save the souls of the natives all the while desecrating the land. I read one time that the fatter the Queens, the more power they would yield so after eating a mammoth meal, slaves would pound their stomachs in an effort to migrate the food through miles of intestinal roads in order to empty the stomach for more consumption. Mavis wore a flowery muumuu that assured me her blood was pumped by the heart of royalty and power.

"Most of the furniture, light fixtures and wall pieces are original to the house," Mavis shared with me as we walked down the upstairs hall. I couldn't help but notice the door to my right that read "Pine Room".

"All the portraits you see are of the Hughes family. Mr. Eugene didn't have nowhere to put all this stuff so he let's Ms. Mary Beth keep it here. Where it belongs anyhow, I reckon," Mavis continued, more than a little out of breath from our climb. She heaved her massive frame into a bedroom on the left that was painted a warm teal color with a hand-painted border of magnolia blooms along the chair rail.

"This is perfect," I said with a sigh. I walked the few feet to the window and opened the plantation shutters. I had guessed right when we turned at the top of the stairs that the room would face the ocean. What a dream!

"Your bathrooms right through the doors here. I quit unpacking folks' suitcases a long time ago when I found some kind of funky stuff in these young folks' suitcase on their honeymoon. I swear to God it looked like a whip or something. Sad thing is, it embarrassed me more than it embarrassed them. Lord, Lord," she said, shaking her head sadly. "Just don't know what the world's done come to."

I giggled behind my hand and pulled her into my arms. It was such a natural thing to do. She reminded me so much of Miss Essie and smelled like butter and flour.

"Thank you, Mavis. Although I'm afraid the most exciting thing you'd find in my suitcase is Tylenol PM," I admitted.

She patted my arm and said, "Thank the Lord for that one. I see you met Mr. Samuel. He's a mess that one. But I reckon he'll be good company for ya. Ya'll just stay out the way of them church ladies. They's a mess now, I tell you what. Come on down around four. Mr. Nathan gonna play his fiddle for we say grace for supper. I've made chicken n dumplings with fresh cream corn and slapped me out some biscuits."

I shut the door behind her as she ambled her way into the hall and took the opportunity to survey my room. It was actually about the size of my bedroom at home, nearly perfectly square. The hardwood floors crawled under the queen sized mahogany bed with an arched canopy draped with lace. A rocking chair swayed slightly in the left corner as I fingered the hand-stitched quilt warming its shoulders. A gas fireplace faced the bed with an oriental throw rug joining their borders. The only other furniture was a double chest of drawers with a secretary made of mahogany, bald cypress and tulip poplar. An engraved metal plate nailed into the tray of the secretary boasted "circa 1832."

I hugged my arms around my chest and swung my shoulders from side to side in an attempt to relieve the tension that settled into my lower back during my siesta on the swing. After hearing the satisfied, "pop", I placed the suitcase on the bed, pulled the straps through the metal hooks and proceeded to unpack my suitcase.

I put my few pairs of shorts in the bottom drawer of the secretary and pulled some hangers from the closet behind the rocking chair. Although my dressiest belongings were a pair of navy slacks and a red, sleeveless turtleneck sweater, I did hang up my t-shirts as well to avoid an all-out rumpled state.

As I re-latched my suitcase and swung it off the bed to place it on the shelf in the closet, I heard something slide around inside. Confident I had unpacked all that I had brought, I lowered the suitcase onto the rocking chair and looked inside.

What I found was a slight tear in the lining, revealing a bulky stack of unopened letters that had worked its way out. On top of the stack was a well-worn piece of paper, yellowing at its edges, folded twice with the simple word *Lily* written on the outside underneath the cracking rubber band that stubbornly completed its job of union. As I carefully unfolded the top note, I lowered myself onto the bed, bending one knee and keeping one foot on the floor, curious to discover who had written to my mother so long ago.

My Dearest Lily:

The letter began. It was dated August 25, 1964. I scanned quickly to the bottom and realized the hurried penmanship belonged to my maternal Irish grandfather Peter O'Reilly, a rather stoic, small built pediatrician that I remembered only from pictures, as he had died two years before I was born. I realized with a start he had actually died within one year of writing this letter. Glancing at the clock and realizing I had at least two hours before dinner, I stuffed two over-sized white shams trimmed with lace behind my back and with my curiosity piqued, began reading the top letter.

My Dearest Lily: *August 25, 1964*
  I write this letter with much trepidation and fear that you will find it. And yet I balance that fear with the hope that you WILL find these letters and begin to realize that I am not the ogre you think I am. Or at least find it in your heart to forgive me for doing what I thought was in your best interest.
  Enclosed you will find several letters written from your young fellow Brady. I'll admit his persistence impressed me. I know now that I should have given you these letters, but in my heart, I believed it best to make a clean break and start new at college.
  So, I am now enclosing them along with this cover letter in the lining of the suitcase, which will carry your belongings to school next week. I will leave it to

fate as to whether he wills you to find them or not. I have interfered enough.

I have great pride in the way you are plowing through the field of your mistakes. I know you will find fertile ground on the other side.

Father

I folded the letter and laid it beside me on the bed. As the stack of letters remained unopened, I could only assume my mother never found them.

I realized the earlier spring rain had returned with a force as I could see its pattern erupt onto the window through the open plantation shutters like an artist throwing paint against a wall. Lightning splintered across the late afternoon sky, and a musty smell had enveloped the room. Having grown up in old homes and antiques, I actually loved the way a rain could wash away the newness of furniture polish and Glade air fresheners to return an older home to its original scent. Not unpleasant, but yet free of the artificial lemony, flowery scent that often polluted the air.

Feeling a little guilty, I hooked my finger under the first letter and forty-five minutes later, longed for the bulging chocolate arms of Miss Essie to rock me against her sagging bosom and say, "Lawd, chile. What we gwine do about dis here?"

Lily,

I don't know where to send this letter because I don't know where you've gone. I am going crazy to find you. I have been to your house twice, but your father just tells me, "Haven't you done enough, son?" and shuts the door in my face.

> *I know I don't have much to offer, but I'm a good person, Lily. You know that. And you know I love you and will work hard to make a good life for you and the baby.*

WHOA! The baby??? I think I actually said that out loud. I continued reading:

> *Please call me or come see me at station. Or I'll meet you anywhere you want. We can get remarried somewhere they can't find us. I don't care. I just need you in my life. I don't know what else to do.*
> *Yours Forever,*
> *Brady*

Each letter was the playbill for the tragic teenage drama of Lily O'Reily and Brady Masion. The couple had apparently dated secretly my mom's senior year of high school as Brady had the audacity to be born to a blue-collar family whose father—gasp—worked at the paper mill. He even committed the carnal sin of articulating his ambitions of one day owning the gas station where he worked to earn money to sneak Mama off to the drive-in movies. I learned from the letters that it was their first sexual experience that resulted in the pregnancy, marriage, annulment, abortion and mama's quick flight to college in Georgia all in about one month's time. Suddenly, cracks ripped down the lining of my memory allowing tiny fingers of understanding to reach through.

My mother, Lilian Baines O'Reilly, was destined for greatness. Her black hair, as black as any night devoid of ambient light and reminiscent of an early Elizabeth Taylor in *Cat on a Hot Tin Roof*, was lustrous and layered. She had amber eyes and a voice that sounded like a gently flowing creek rippling over a bed of mossy covered rocks, winding its way around drawn out syllables. And I knew from the few late night arguments that permeated the pillow covering my head that she was the spoiled only child of two people whose most important daily ritual was chiseling out the perfection of their daughter.

Or so that was what my father threw around our house on the rare occasion he dared stand up to my mother. That is until a drunk driver silenced his rantings forever when my mother stormed out of the house after a particularly bad argument and shrouded my father in a lifetime of guilt.

Fortunately, she was the drunk driver, and the only other casualty was the guardrail that banned her descent over the shoulder of Highway 41 S. Seatbelts were not mandatory at that time, and she plunged through the front windshield like it was a spider web. That bend in the road was more of a tombstone to me growing up than her actual gravesite for I paid silent homage to a woman I barely knew every morning on my way to high school.

Closing the last letter, I realized that in this short span of time, I had learned more about my mother than in the fifteen years I had sought her love. But knowledge and understanding were more like distant cousins than actual siblings, and I had no idea how to process this information. I needed Miss Essie and yearned for her like a child reaches for its security blanket in the dead of the night to silence nightmares and bring life to dreams.

I sat there in my silence, hugging my knees to my chest, wondering how to relate this sudden sympathy and sadness to the woman I spent my entire childhood trying to make smile.

I was surprised to learn later that Daddy knew all along about Brady Masion and everything associated with him. I remember him sitting in his burgundy, tattered Lazy Boy recliner, sipping his nightly bourbon and coke. After he read the letters I had laid on his lap, he rolled his head up and said sadly, "Your mama told me about all of this right before she got pregnant with you. I just thought I could love her enough for both of us."

He went on to say she didn't even want children; how she felt she didn't deserve one. He spent the rest of my childhood trying to convince her she did.

Unsure of how much time I spent on the bed, I swung my legs and glanced in the mirror hanging over the bedside table. I hastily ran a comb through my shoulder-length hair and twisted it into an over-sized clip. Hoping my rumpled state was okay for Mavis' chicken n dumplings, I grabbed my cell phone and hurried downstairs.

I found Samuel standing just under the stairs, silently peaking around the corner. Without turning, he shushed me by waving his hand behind his back. He had changed to faded Levi's and a yellow polo shirt with Birkenstocks on his feet. I crept closer and looked over his shoulder at the carnival atmosphere exhibited in the dining room. It was a scene right out of that special I watched on A&E about PT Barnum & Bailey Circus.

"What is going on?" I whispered, as a dapper man in a Panama hat and a silver goatee began playing the harmonica, and another lady that looked like a blonde Delta Burke's mother with a sunburned face in an oversized t-shirt emblazoned with "Grandkids Spoiled Here" tapped spoons on her hot pink stretch pants. About a dozen more gathered around clapping their hands.

The table was a rectangle mahogany that seated twenty with two silver candelabras flanking steaming dishes placed on black wrought iron trivets. You could smell a faint odor of boiled chicken smothered in black pepper and lemons, but the fresh baked biscuits nestled in a wiregrass basket teased my nose before I ever walked into the dining room.

"That, my friend, is the Sunset Group from Gainesville, GA," he whispered back. "Let's get in there before Nathan starts playing the fiddle, or we may miss our seats."

Saying grace was a veritable honky tonk festival with Nathan fiddling "I'll Fly Away" while we sat at the table, stood behind the table or just lounged in the love seats and gentleman's chairs that lined one wall. I was passed from one embrace to the next as each member lapped his or her generous attention on me.

I didn't grow up with physical affection and rarely heard the words I love you unless there were witnesses present. But through gritted determination, I forged my way out of those habits and lavished hugs and kisses to anyone who would not have me arrested in my adult life. Rob's family helped me a lot in this. I remembered the first time I met his mother, Debra, in the kitchen of his ranch-style home.

"Well, it's about time you brought this girl to meet me as much as you've been talking about her. Come here, darling, and give me a hug," she said, wiping her hands on her red and white checkered apron and walking towards me.

I slipped an arm around her waist and sort of leaned into her embrace.

"What is this? Girl, someone needs to teach you how to hug properly. This is how we hug in this house." She turned me to face her, put both of my hands around her ample waist and wrapped her arms around my shoulders, drowning me in the smell of lemon pine sol and grease. I never wanted it to end.

So I kissed and slobbered right back with the best of them at Serenity Point, and after being passed back to my seat beside

Mary Beth who sat at the foot of the table, I was deemed an honorary member of the Sunset Club.

After the last pull of the bow across the strings, we gave a unanimous AMEN and pulled our white cloth napkins embroidered with SP from our plates and began to pass the dishes. The silence was deafening after our explosion of sound that preceded dinner, but the only noise resounding now was the clink of silver serving utensils being returned to dishes as they circumnavigated the table.

As bellies began to fill up, the conversation sprang out, and I learned more about my weekend compatriots. To the right of Nathan sat the Panama Hat man whose name was Arthur Boatwright, and who was the self-appointed narrator of the group.

"I'm a retired aristocrat, you see. Not much to look at, but got me a helluva lot of money my kids don't know about. Me and the Misses started buying stock when we first got married sixty-something years ago in the products we used—like Coca Cola, Proctor and Gamble and so forth. Gonna spend as much as we can for we go see our maker," he said with a grin, elbowing the perky lady to his left.

And on around the table he went. Mrs. Boatwright was as tiny as Mary Beth was large, but complained about the fact she couldn't keep any weight on anymore. I couldn't wait to be old enough to agonize over the weight I lost rather than gained!

The names blurred together, but the camaraderie was clear and once again, I basked in the unfamiliarity of unabashed affection and love. I had yearned for this my entire life, even before our marriage counselor had articulated my desires out loud.

"Melanie needs you to show her you appreciate her, Rob, in her ways not yours. Women aren't as likely to feel loved just because they feel financially and physically secure," Linda Sadler would tell us several years ago in her camel-colored tailored suit, pushing her black-framed glasses on her nose with her pointer finger.

I looked at him expectantly, waiting for his response. But since he had agreed to come under his own terms—listen and not comment—his silence wasn't unexpected. We were the classic passive-aggressive relationship. I was the aggressor, always throwing words around trying to get a reaction. Rob was more passive, not even hearing the counselor suggest to him that I needed more than a roof over my head to feel secure and loved.

Rob never got that. He thought by paying the bills, allowing me to stay home with the kids and basically adopting a hunt and kill caveman mentality then that should be enough. He would constantly ask me why I couldn't be happy with our life, and for the life of me, I didn't know why. We thankfully never faced any serious illnesses in those we loved. We were financially enough secure, relatively attractive people. There was nothing on the exterior to give any cause for my restlessness. And yet its mere existence made my frustrations that much worse because I couldn't articulate a reason for it. I was just simply lost.

In the one session he agreed to attend, he looked like a protestant visiting Catholic Mass, in awe of the ritualistic peeling of the emotional layers of our marriage and struck dumb by Linda's vast vocabulary of psychological terms as if she was a priest intoning Latin.

My mother died the year before I met Rob so he never witnessed the effect of her lacking affections on my childhood. My mother lived vicariously through me. I was a veteran of twelve county beauty pageants by the time I was five.

She would roll out of bed, drape her silk bath robe fringed in faux fur across her freckled, pale shoulders and begin to play the most distinguished role of her most undistinguished day— dressing me for school. There were rare times that I caught a glimpse of affection for me when she would hold me back at arms-length and tilt her head to the side. A slight smile would play at the corners of her mouth as she fussed with my hair. That is until her eyes would travel down to my protruding stomach, my belly button peaking out between the end of my shirt and my pants that I had pulled down beneath it so I could breathe. I could then see a look of disgust cloud her vision as she would jerk the hem of my shirt down over the rolls of dimpled skin that resembled cottage cheese. It was through her eyes that I would view myself in every mirror for the rest of my life.

It was her death that liberated my life, and I wore a t-shirt to her funeral. I took red velvet cake to my bedroom when the funeral party adjourned to our house. I ate the entire thing and promptly stuck my finger down my throat to throw it up—a practice I would come to repeat many times in my adolescence. I didn't come out for two days, and no one thought to look for me. My father was just worn out from the war that was their marriage with a flag of surrender that draped across her casket in white roses.

A clinking of a silver knife against a crystal water goblet dragged me to the present.

"I'd like to make a toast to our new guest," Nathan shouted. He always spoke as though we all wore earmuffs. "Miss Melanie, we are so glad you are here. We hope Serenity Point permeates your spirit and nestles into your bones so that even when you are away, you are always truly home."

"Here, here," the group rang out, and we touched glasses. I had to lift up slightly in my chair to touch Samuel's outstretched glass that reached across from me. He was looking at me curiously as though reading my thoughts, so I gave him a quick smile. He returned my smile, but with a slight upturn of his right eyebrow.

After we took several helpings of dinner, much to the delight of Mavis who moved around us like a bulldozer intent on replenishing a landfill, Mrs. Marion Beecham of the hot pink capris fame, jumped up and began taking up everyone's plates.

"Go on, Mavis, I know you got that fresh peach cobbler warming in that oven. I'll get these plates. Come on, Samuel, darling, you can help me." She winked at Samuel, giving him a flirty smile.

Mrs. Beecham was a widow of twenty years who used to dance the Cancan in several off-off-Broadway productions in New York City in the thirties. She moved with a sensual grace and enunciated each word carefully and loudly as if projecting from center stage. Her long pink acrylic nails clinked against the plates as she almost pirouetted around the table. Samuel had confessed earlier to being a little in love with her.

Nathan retrieved his fiddle from his case and gently pulled the bow in tune. Mr. Boatwright took his cue, bringing his harmonica to his lips and in beautiful harmony began to play "The Old Rugged Cross." The smell of peach cobbler wove around the room, and our already full stomachs rumbled again with desire. The sweet odor of cigar danced contentedly with the aroma of fresh brewed coffee, and we silently listened to several more of the old hymns.

I eased my chair away from the table and silently made my way to kiss Mavis on the cheek with a whisper of "I enjoyed it" in her ear. The setting sun behind Serenity Point beckoned me to join it as we said goodbye to yet another Florida Friday.

I settled myself into the rocking chair on the side porch with the setting sun swaying gently behind me and the sound of a darkening ocean rolling back out to the sea as if someone spilled a jar of black ink. You couldn't see the ocean from the porch, but you could hear the sea gulls as they danced across the sand looking for their own desserts.

I realized with a start that I had not called my kids, so I retrieved my cell phone from the pocket of my gray cable knit sweater I had carried down for this very purpose and dialed my home.

It was about 6 p.m. in Alabama, but no one answered after four rings. Odd, I thought. Allie usually barreled after a ringing phone like she was running through Times Square on New Year's Eve. I hung up and redialed. This time, KitKat answered the phone.

"Hey, sweet girl. How's it shaking?" I asked lightly.

"Hey, back, Mom. Sorry I couldn't get to the phone. Will hid it behind the sofa," she replied. "How's it going with you?"

"Not too bad. It's really relaxing, especially after I stuffed myself with chicken n dumplings and peach cobbler. I hope I can make it up the stairs to bed, I'm so full."

"Don't rub it in. I just heated up a bowl of spaghettios for Will and me. I think Allie had a pop tart."

I next asked the expected rhetorical question. "Where's your father?"

"Hadn't heard from him. But it's cool, Mom. Allie actually stayed home all day for a change, and Will and I played UNO and watched some TV. We're all right. When are you coming home?" She asked with a slight catch in her voice.

I had never bad-mouthed Rob to the children, and I wasn't going to start now. I reined in my temper like a cowboy roping a steer and replied, "I appreciate all your help, KitKat. I'm very proud of you. Dad should be home soon, and I'll be home about mid-afternoon on Sunday. I love you, honey, and I'll try to call you tomorrow."

"Okay, Mom. Call me tomorrow. Love you too," she said, hanging up the phone.

I pressed the off button on my cell phone and laid it against my tensed forehead for a minute. All my anger from this morning welled up inside me. Suddenly, I reared back and threw my cell phone against the wall, narrowly missing Samuel as he rounded the corner.

Chapter 10

It was fun watching Melanie's reaction to the Sunset Club. I could tell she was very uneasy with the instantaneous combination of noise and affection, but I admired how quickly she collected herself.

I had spent the afternoon thinking of her, which surprised me in that I hadn't given more than a passing thought to anyone other than my own grief and myself since Sarah died.

"Do you think you'll ever want to date again?" My oldest brother Tom had asked me several months after the funeral. He had moved to Gwinnett County after college, and we met in a bar in Buckhead to watch the Georgia Tech game one Saturday. I wasn't particularly interested in the game, as I had attended the state university in Georgia for both my undergraduate and law degrees. But it was nice to cocoon myself in the noise and smoke that was the standard stage for sports bars. I was the youngest of the three, and there was always a protective nature to their relationship with me.

Tom was the biggest of us. While only about five foot ten inches, his weight consistently hovered around 225. But he had the biggest heart and cried like a little girl who lost her puppy at every sappy movie our mom forced on us. Today, he had a slight sheen of sweat on his upper lip, his dark hair damp from perspiration, but with love and concern in his eyes. We were oblivious to the smoke and clinks of the beer bottles or the eruptions of noise persistent in the crowded bar.

I leaned back in my chair and ran my fingers through my hair. "I don't know how to do that, Tom. It is amazing now to know how much of my life was filled with her. I didn't realize it while I had her. And now that I don't, I don't know how to be. And it kills me to know how few times I told her that."

Tom seemed to consider that for a minute. "I think she knew. She used to always call you her little workaholic, but it was always with a sense of humor. Don't sell yourself too short, little brother. Sarah knew how driven you were, how dedicated you were. She knew how much you loved her, too, with that same sort of obsession. Somehow, you've got to know that."

"I do know that, but I'll regret every minute I didn't spend with her; every second I don't get to touch her. Man, do you know how hard it was to see her in that coffin at the viewing? All those people walking up to me telling me how beautiful she looked, how natural. What a joke! All I wanted to do was crawl inside and lay beside her. Just so I could touch her again. I just can't stand the thought of not touching her again." I looked up at the ceiling and widened my eyes to avoid the collecting tears from falling down my face.

Tom reached over and in his typical sensitive fashion, put his hand over mine and stroked the top with his thumb. Tom was the only one of us that was never ashamed to show his feelings in public. "I'm not going to tell you I know how you feel, because I don't. Hell, I can't even date a girl more than a few months without feeling like I can't breathe. But not you, man. You got so much love left to give because Sarah taught you how to do that. She taught you how to love. Even if you don't ever love that way again, at least don't close yourself off to that possibility. If not for yourself, at least do that for Sarah."

What would Tom think about this fascination I had with

Melanie? Not in a physical sense, but more of curiosity. What brought her here? And why was she alone? I had noticed a simple gold wedding band, but that was her only adornment. She didn't appear flashy, very conservative in her dress, and yet she was quick with her retorts while we walked up from the beach.

I used the opportunity at dinner to flirt with Mrs. Beecham a little more. She had such a sexy little wink whenever she finished a sentence that it was almost like her personal punctuation mark. I was understandably disappointed when I noticed her flirtatiousness was more a characteristic than by design toward me, but enjoyed the attention nonetheless. I was thrilled when she asked me to help her clear the table as it gave me a front row seat to the best sashay in the business.

As I was walking into the kitchen, a movement caught the corner of my eye. I noticed Melanie getting up quietly from the table while the others were served the peach cobbler. She silently made her way around the corner, whispered briefly to Mavis, the resident housekeeper/chef and left out of the rear door by the kitchen.

Intrigued, I returned to the dining table after helping Mrs. Beecham in the kitchen, but decided to give her a few minutes before I tried to find out the answers to some of my questions. Sarah used to tell me I had an insatiable curiosity that served me well as an attorney, but often annoyed more reserved people in casual settings. I was willing to take that chance here, as I had learned all I needed to know about my elderly companions and really just wanted someone to talk with on any subject other than the marvels of over-the-counter heartburn medicine.

After about ten minutes, I slipped quietly back into the kitchen and retrieved a bottle of chardonnay from the wine rack.

"Don't get that. It's not even chilled," Mavis admonished me from the swinging kitchen door, her right hand on the small of her back, her left full of dessert plates.

"Lord, the sugar and the pressure done got me tonight, Mister Samuel. Here, chile, you take this one out of the bucket. Let Mavis get you two glasses, and you go find out how to put a real smile on that chile's face, ya hear?" She huffed at me expectantly.

"You noticed it too?"

"Sure did. That chile can smile a smile to light up a room. But that light don't reach her eyes. Breaks my heart to see someone so pretty be so unhappy."

I was glad to know it wasn't my own imagination, but Mavis' observations only fueled my curiosity. "Me, too. Believe me, I have seen unhappiness in my own mirror every day for the past year. She's stronger with her feelings than I am. At least she makes an attempt to keep them hidden or at least to herself. I never did that." I had told Mavis all about Sarah one night after drinking too much moonshine with Uncle Jesse. He was the local caretaker that lived in a small house down the beach and played his fiddle every night while lubricating his picking fingers with some homemade moonshine.

Mavis was a wonderful counselor on loss. Her own husband had died of a heart attack in his early thirties leaving her with two small children. That was more than forty years ago, and she said there still wasn't a day that she didn't shed a tear for him.

"Oh, Mr. Samuel, you been grieving just fine. You've just got to learn how to grieve while you live. Trust me, you can do both. You don't have to do one or the other. Sounds like Miss Melanie might need to learn that too."

It never occurred to me that Melanie was in mourning. "You think someone died?" I asked.

"I don't rightly know about that, but I suspect not. She got that beat down look, like life done let her down. Or someone. She looks like she's grieving for life, not loss. But you go and find out. I suspect she'll tell you in due time. Just turn on the charm like you do with them old ladies, and she'll open on up to you. Now scoot."

I leaned in and kissed her on the cheek. She swatted me with her towel, turned back towards the sink and started humming "The Old Rugged Cross" while she began to rinse off the dessert plates that she brought into the kitchen.

I glanced up the staircase on my way down the hall, but betted against her going to bed so early. I looked to my left into the sitting room and noticed a faint outline of someone on the side porch through the window. I let myself out of the front door; quietly easing the screened door shut and stepped around the corner of the house. I quickly jerked my head back as a cell phone came hurling towards me, barely missing my head.

Chapter 11

"Samuel, I am so sorry," I said in horror, jumping up to retrieve my splintered phone from the wooden floor of the porch.

"I'm just curious what that cell phone did to you. I know reception sucks out here, but don't you think you should cut it some slack?" He asked seriously, leaning against the corner wall of the house.

Breaking out into laughter, I gestured for him to join me in the settee across from my rocker. He took his wire-rimmed glasses from his nose and lifting the bottom of his untucked polo shirt, wiped the humidity from the lenses.

"I won't ask what dire event resulted in the demise of said cell phone, but you have me curious. Who would have guessed such a temper could reside under that buttoned-up, starchy shirt?

"You know, they say still waters run deep. What's your story?" He prompted, settling into the deep cushions that threatened to swallow him whole.

"Let's just hope I don't have to resort to the brass knuckles in my bra," I said jokingly. Where did that come from? I don't think I had ever hinted at the word bra to a man before in my life, not even my husband. Something about this guy just absolutely disarmed me.

"What is it you want to know?"

"Are you avoiding the question? Come on; tell Uncle Samuel all your dirty secrets. Anyone that carries brass knuckles and hurls cell phones at unsuspecting passers-by must harbor some good ones," he said crossing his left ankle over his right knee.

Without hesitation, I said, "Well, let's see. I've been married to Rob Graham for sixteen years. We got married when I was twenty-one, and he was twenty-two…"

"That would make you…" he interrupted.

"Old enough, thank you very much," I said, wagging my finger at him like the old school teacher I was. "Anyway, I've got three children. Allie is fifteen and determined to prematurely gray my hair. Katherine is eight and exactly like me, too old for her age. Will is six and has yet to experience life in the real world. We like to say he exists in 'Will World' much to the challenge of his kindergarten teacher."

"Sounds like a full house," Samuel replied. "But you didn't answer my question."

"What else did you want to know?" I asked confused.

"I asked you to tell me about yourself."

"I did," I said stubbornly. Who exactly was this guy?

"No, you didn't. You told me about your husband. You told me about your children. But unless that totally defines Melanie Graham, there's a lot you left out, my new friend. Come on, what makes Melanie tick?" He asked gently, leaning toward me with both elbows on his knees.

With stunning clarity I realized Samuel had just unknowingly spotlighted my entire issues with myself. No one had ever gone beyond the initial question of my identity, seemingly content with allowing me to envelope myself in the personalities of my family. I honestly didn't know how to respond.

The breeze slid up over the ocean and rustled the pampas grass generating the only sound for a few moments. Samuel looked at me thoughtfully while my emotions played out on my face. I lowered my head and considered my response.

Finally, I looked up at him and said, "Honestly, Samuel, I don't know how to answer that question. I've been sitting here trying to think of some witty response to salvage whatever pride I might have. But the fact of the matter is, I lost myself a long time ago, and I don't know how to find me. That is betting that I ever knew who I was to begin with." I embarrassed myself by promptly bursting into tears, but made no move to wipe them away as they dropped heavily onto my folded hands.

"I'm sorry. I didn't mean to pry or to make you cry. But honestly, from the moment I saw you chasing after that red bird looking like you just woke up, to the way you rubbed Mrs. Turner's shoulders at dinner when she complained of arthritis, I just wanted to know more about you. Surely, you must remember a time when you had a dream about your life, Mel," he said easily, but with a slightly shocked expression at my outburst as most men do with female tears. "Tell me about little Melanie whatever your last name was. What did she like to do?"

"You mean what did I like to do or what was I allowed to do?" I asked cynically. And so I told him.

I described the little girl who left the house on Christmas break in her shining patent leather shoes, white stockings and matching red velour pants and sweater. I told about the girl who ran straight to Miss Essie's house and outlined the proper Melanie onto the rickety brass bed, aligning the sweater, pants and stockings as if she were taking a nap. Then that little girl coagulated into the real Mel by sliding her head through a t-shirt and jogging pants that Miss Essie bought at K-mart and kept freshly laundered at her house. The outfit smelled like soap and fresh air, and I would pull my hair into a ponytail and meet my best friend in the kitchen to make fried pies.

I told him about winning the argument to play lassie league softball, which in hindsight was less about acquiescing to my demands, and more about my mother's chance to regularly confer with my coach, Mr. Johnson. I learned after her death that he was her first affair during the summer between third and fourth grades.

I told Samuel about my need to make people feel good. How the only time my mama would let me touch her was when I spent hours brushing her long, luxurious black hair. I told him about her rages if I came home without a bow in my hair—even in the fourth grade.

I told him about her death.

"Where was your father growing up?" He interceded when I took a breath.

"Oh, he would pop in around eight at night, but run to the television set in order to keep peace by ignoring the issues. My mother was absolutely gorgeous and won the freshman beauty pageant at the college in north Georgia where they met. He fell for her hook, line and sinker and convinced her he was from big timber money and could keep her in the lifestyle that she was well acquainted," I told him.

"Although what he said was true, what he neglected to mention was he was paying his own way through college because he wanted to study agriculture, cow farming to be exact and had no desire to broker timber with Granddaddy."

Daddy married Mama and had her pregnant before he took her to Sewanee to meet his parents. Although his family loved him, there was no question he was on his own because of his choices. I realized after reading her letters earlier that she probably married him to punish her parents for forcing her to leave the love of her life.

"Years later he told me he would never forget the look on

mama's face when his daddy patted him on the back and told him good luck and give us a shout when the baby comes. Daddy finished college at a smaller school near our hometown, and Mama stayed home to raise me."

"Your poor Mama," Samuel said. "She must have been devastated."

I looked over my right shoulder and allowed the blackness of the night to swallow my response for a minute.

"Probably. I don't think living in a two-bedroom shanty two feet from the railroad was her idea of happily ever after. But Daddy did all right. When farming couldn't pay the bills, he opened a clothing store in town, too proud to ask his parents for money. He made a decent living out of that and farmed on the weekends. He moved us to the other side of town by the time I was three. But Mama spent the rest of my childhood trying to rub that railroad grease out of my skin, both literally and figuratively.

"After her death, Daddy focused all the attention that went unnoticed with my mother on me. We played ball, he took me fishing, I wrapped presents at the store during Christmas breaks, and he paid me to pitch the hay for the cows in the winter. But as close as we were, he never could bring himself to show me any affection. I can't remember him ever telling me he loved me. Love didn't play fair with daddy so I guess he was a little gun-shy of playing the game."

When I looked back at Samuel, I was struck silent by the fact that he had not moved. It didn't even appear that he had batted an eye for his attention was totally and completely on me. It was almost as if he had blocked out an entire world and narrowed it only to include the two of us. I didn't want to share with him yet about my afternoon findings for fear he would think I was completely crazy. But somehow the simplicity of his company wrapped me in a blanket of peacefulness I had never felt. I had just shared more with him than with anyone in my life.

Maybe it was the added benefit that our only audience was the ocean breaking on the shore and the crickets conversing with the frogs to distract our conversation. Whatever it was, I felt a tremendous burden lift from my shoulders as I slumped back in my chair to try to regulate my breathing.

"Isn't it a bitch to grow up and realize your parents aren't perfect? But isn't it nice to grow up to get a better perception of their imperfections?" He asked wisely. "I grew up with Ozzie and Harriett, and luckily they remained that way even after I moved on, got married and grew up. But I do know even they aren't perfect and neither am I. And neither, my friend, are you.

"Sounds like your mom tried hard to make you perfect instead of embracing your individuality. I would imagine when you were onstage with all your other five-year-old beauty queens that there weren't any differences among you. Dwarfed clones forced to parade across the stage of the vicariousness of their southern mothers. And, unfortunately for your mom, it was at those moments she felt her greatest pride, and you felt your closest relationship."

"What are you, Sigmund Freud?" I asked, tears freely running down my cheeks. "If your parents were so perfect, how are you so insightful to dysfunction?"

"Because what I loved most about my wife was her ability to be imperfect. She never apologized for a dirty house, piled up laundry or the gas gauge being too low in her beat-up Jeep Cherokee. But what she gave freely and without abandon was her love of life, and it infected anyone around her," he said dreamily.

"Where is she now, staying home with all your kids so you can play pseudo psychiatry with me?" I asked haughtily.

"No, she died a year ago," he said with a matter-of-fact tone. "She was thirty-five years old and bled to death internally before we ever knew she had a stroke. Nobody's fault. She never told anyone she was dizzy or had headaches because she wasn't one to complain. She kept going to work at the pre-school, and it wasn't until her funeral that her co-workers told me she would lay down during snack time in the teacher's lounge with a cold rag. And I was too busy being Mr. Hot Shot Lawyer to come home at a decent hour and recognize that things weren't as they should be."

I listened in horror as he spoke of coming home three hours later than he had promised one weeknight only to find her slumped over the kitchen table. He didn't wait for an ambulance, but called 911 on his cell phone with her draped over his shoulder as he rushed out the door of their Atlanta townhouse. A police car met him a couple of miles up the road and with lights flashing escorted him the ten miles to the nearest emergency room. By then it was too late. She was pronounced dead before they ever put her in a room.

"They told me later she was probably dead when we left the house. It took me a long time to get over the fact I had my dead wife over my shoulder," he said, unashamedly wiping the tears pouring down his face, holding his glasses in his left hand. When he cleared his eyes, all that remained was raw, naked pain. He admitted to lying to his parents about where he was going this weekend.

"The anniversary of her death was yesterday. They wanted me to spend the week with them in the mountains. I just really wanted to be alone. So, I told them I had a client to see in Florida and not to worry that I had a full agenda to keep me busy. But I really cleared my calendar and came here this week because Sarah once told me she wanted to spend some time at a bed and breakfast on the ocean. We never did. So now I am doing it in her memory hoping she can guide me in my next steps. I know I'm too young to become a eunuch. But I feel like I need her permission to act my age again. I'm only thirty-eight, but I've been acting like I could be the founding member of the Sunset Group in there," he said, tossing his head toward the house.

"Oh my, Samuel. I am so sorry. How could you let me go on and on about my poor pitiful childhood without letting me know your pain," I gasped. I got up from my rocker and sat beside him on the settee, putting my hand on his knee.

"One thing I learned from Sarah, there is no pain on earth greater than another. It is relevant and potent to each person no matter what it is, and there is no measuring stick. Yes, her death gutted me, and I was a virtual ghost of myself for many months. But I was being unfaithful to her spirit of life and knew she would be tremendously disappointed in me. So I am here to ask her forgiveness and rejoin the living. One change I did make is that I gave up corporate law, and now I spend my time defending the poor and downtrodden. Pretty noble, wouldn't you say?" He asked, visibly collecting himself.

I nodded, unsure of how to respond.

"Look, Mel, I didn't tell you all that to make you feel bad. I think you have barely scratched the surface of your life story to me. I hope you will tell me more. You remind me of Sarah in a way. She was so easy to talk to and as easy to look at as you are. But somehow you have forgotten who you are and what you want in life. And I learned from Sarah that is a wasted life. So, tell me, what do you want to be when you grow up?"

He bent one knee up on the cushion and propped his elbow behind his head, holding his head up with one hand. He patted my hand encouragingly.

We talked for what seemed like minutes, but was actually

three hours. Mary Beth had poked her head around the corner a couple of times to see if we needed some refreshments and discreetly sat a pitcher of sweet tea and two frosty mugs beside the door.

One benefit of sharing accommodations with the elderly was their early bedtime. We heard a chorus of goodnights ring through the walls and pictured the group making its way up the stairs. Only Mr. and Mrs. Habernathy had the downstairs bedroom, which was handicapped accessible due to Mr. Habernathy's knee surgery and his wife's asthmatic conditions. We collectively held our breaths, hoping they would bypass their goodnights to us, and so they did.

Around ten o'clock, Samuel glanced at his watch, and then asked, "How about a walk on the beach?"

Without hesitation, I replied, "Love to." Wrapping my sweater back around my shoulders, I kicked off my shoes and walked down the steps to join Samuel on the natural path rolling over the dunes.

The night was inked in dark blue with outlining clouds wrinkling the surface of a perfectly round moon. The stars were blanketed by the lingering thunderclouds although the rain had quieted during dinner. You could see distant lightning as we made our way south, but could hear no thunder. It was almost like watching a silent movie as the clouds conversed with one another through the lights. We walked for some time without saying a word, our voices exhausted from the previous three-hour epiphanies our emotions had endured.

Samuel's hands began in his pockets, his feet still in their sandals, kicking the sand around his rolled up blue jeans as we slowly crunched our way along the sand the earlier rain had patted down. At some point, his hands dropped to his side, his right hand occasionally knocking my left as we unconsciously aligned our steps. I don't even know at what point he took my hand, but it never occurred to me not to let him. There was nothing untoward about the act. I never felt threatened or the slightest bit guilty. We were just two people wrapped in the pain of our past, reconciling its influences into the character of the present and pondering its impact on the future.

Chapter 12

The rising sun threaded through the shutters way too early on Saturday morning. I turned into my pillow to steal a few more minutes of sleep when I heard the steady thump of a walking cane march its way down the hall.

"Geriatrics," I muttered to myself. I forgot that early to bed also meant early to rise for my elderly friends.

"I hope that colored lady has some more of those biscuits for breakfast. Of course, that peach cobbler didn't sit too well with me all night," a craggy feminine voice spoke through my wall as they made their way down the hall.

"Well, Irma, if you hadn't had two pieces with that ice cream you probably wouldn't need those Alka Seltzers," her companion replied. Their voices grew more muffled as I heard them creak down the stairs.

Fully awake now, I lifted my arms over my head to stretch, sending blood flowing through my body and nudging the rest of my limbs to life. Reluctantly, I threw back the covers, found my slippers and walked around the bed to the bathroom. Passing the door, I noticed an unfolded piece of pink Serenity Point stationery with a smaller folded note lying just inside the door.

My knees popped as I bent the retrieve both notes. I smiled to myself as I read the handwritten itinerary.

SP
Good morning:

I hope you enjoyed a beautiful rest in our Magnolia Room. There is coffee just outside your door on the butler's tray. The following is our meal times and menu items:

7:30 a.m. until 9

Mavis has fixed a breakfast buffet for you to eat at your leisure. The buffet includes scrambled eggs, fresh blueberry muffins and of course, her hand tossed biscuits.

12 p.m.

Mavis will be fixing chicken salad sandwiches, tuna casserole, corn pudding and summer vegetables to be served on the veranda. If you decide to go to town, just tell Mavis to fix you a basket.

6 p.m.

Mavis is delighting us tonight with smothered pork chops, broccoli risotto and sweet potato biscuits. Don't miss the pecan crunch pie!

I hope you have a wonderful day. If you don't like anything on the menu, just let me know!
Love,
Mary Beth

Good grief! Just reading that menu got my stomach growling in anticipation. I started toward the bathroom when I remembered the second note. Written in handwriting closely resembling a doctor's hurried penmanship, Samuel wrote

Mel:

What do you say we hit the town today? I really enjoyed last night so much and would like to continue our conversations today. I found some interesting things on my ventures last week. Meet me on the porch at 8:30 if you're game.
Samuel

I glanced quickly at the clock and realized it was nudging on eight already so I bolted to the bathroom. No quick shower in a house subtitled, "What's Ya Hurry?" so I turned the faucets on the claw-foot tub on full thrust and threw off my clothes. I jumped in without waiting for the tub to fill-up and immersed my head under the running tap.

Ten minutes later, I stumbled into my black shorts and a white crew neck, short sleeve t-shirt with brightly colored flip flops embroidered as if elves marched across my front. I thought briefly about calling the kids, but then remembered the remnants of my phone in the garbage can. Mentally promising to call them from town, I grabbed my purse and strode out of the room.

I almost fell over the promised coffee in the hall and praising all the Columbian gods that created this miracle, I poured a large cup, generously pouring in cream and sugar. I noticed no light shining under the Pine Room door so I ran down the stairs.

The only sound of the morning was the clink of dishes and the distant hum of a dishwasher. Seeing no one to greet good morning, I slipped out of the front door after grabbing two biscuits to the welcoming arms of the Saturday sunshine and salty air.

"Typical man," I thought to myself as I glanced at my watch

that read 8:48 with no sight of Samuel. I lowered myself into the swing on which I had made acquaintance the day before. Swinging slightly with the breeze and breathing in the scent of honeysuckle, I thought again about the letters to my mother. Whoever this Brady Masion was, he certainly had a flair for words, which I'm sure appealed to my mother's rather dramatic nature. The last letter written was particularly poignant, and I practically knew it from memory:

My Dearest Lily:

I guess my letters are a waste of time, so I'll send you this last one hoping one day you will find it. My heart is broken for our baby and us. I found out from your mother that you were forced to have that abortion. I knew that had to be the case when Jimmy Stinson told me you did. I was praying he was wrong altogether, but I knew in my heart you would never agree to kill our baby. She said you had gone away to school, but would not tell me where. At least she told me that much and only because your Dad wasn't home. I think she said he was having some sort of tests run at the hospital.

Lily, I would have worked my fingers to the bone to give you both a good life. One thing you would never have to worry about was love because I had more than enough to last a lifetime. Always will no matter where our lives lead us. I hope you will find happiness with someone. Someone who will appreciate your willful spirit, smell the sweet perfume of your skin and lose himself in your long, black hair that seems to go on and on. Your sense of humor will make many laugh, your sensitivity will hold back many tears.

Whoever you are with in your happily ever after, I pray that you will give me a passing thought. For you will always be the love of my life.
  All my love forever,
  Brady

I tried hard to picture my mother laughing. All I could recall was that throaty sound she would make when she threw back her head at some witty remark made by any unremarkable man in her presence. But I now had a glimpse at the cause of her insecurity, her driving need to wash away her pain with wine and whiskey and the desperation to purify herself through creating the perfect daughter.

I remembered seeing her crying on the front porch of our home one night. I guess I was about seven or eight, old enough to remember, but too young to understand. She was wearing a white satin nightgown with delicate spaghetti straps almost as thin as dental floss, sitting on the front steps, silently sobbing into her hands. Her feet were bare, and I remember thinking her toes must be cold. I ran back inside to retrieve her slippers from her closet. I crept out the front door and silently placed her slippers beside her on the steps. She never acknowledged my presence, and I tiptoed back to bed.

Looking back, there were many times I can now recall her going off into her own world, probably grieving for the baby she was not allowed to love and the boy she did. She always came back, but in her last years, she seemed to go away more and more for longer periods of time.

I knew firsthand the guilt associated with abortion. In the two years I taught school, I was the director of the after-school program. During my last year, I became close to a sixteen-year-old African American girl named Samantha who worked with us. She was absolutely stunning, bright in every way. She had olive skin and cat eyes that changed color depending on her mood. And she was pregnant.

Her boyfriend was some punk that was regularly marched to the principal's office for any and all offenses, but said all the right words to Samantha. Prior to the pregnancy, she confided in me that she was willing to go all the way with the punk—I can't even remember his name that is how insignificant he was to society and a complete waste of DNA. But Samantha loved him. Because I wasn't allowed to discuss birth control with the kids, I gently encouraged her to talk to her mother before making any decisions.

One month later, she was crying in my room, asking me to help her administer the drugstore pregnancy test. And blaring at us like a foghorn in a storm was the plus sign in the window. I ached for her as she stumbled out of the room as once again, I was encumbered by the politics of public education. I could not discuss religion, sex or even emotions. We were merely stoic robots regurgitating the state mandated curriculum with no sense of flesh and bone, much less the souls of our students.

I ran into Samantha one late afternoon in the fall as I pushed KitKat in the swing at the city park. You have to look fast to catch fall in the South, but if you caught a glimpse, it was a visionary feast to savor. The temperature hovered around sixty-five in the late afternoon, and the breeze rustled the scarlet, green and golden leaves to blanket the ground. Samantha was babysitting her four-year-old brother so we let them play in the sandbox while we sat on the wooden bench to catch up.

"Mrs. Graham, I just want you to know how much I appreciated your help this past year with my situation," she said with tears in her eyes, but in her normal articulate voice. "But my dad flipped out when I told him. He wouldn't even let me tell Roderick about the baby."

"What happened, honey?" I asked, gently stroking her arm that lay across the back of the park bench. She was still so pretty, but her eyes spoke of an unmentionable pain. I reached up to wipe a tear off the tip of her upturned nose.

She told me her mother took her to get an abortion two weeks after our talk. I knew something was happening because she didn't come back to the after-school program. I didn't want to ask around because I feared it would only fuel the gossip sure to spread the halls of the high school quicker than a lit match in hell.

She went into detail about the counselor at the clinic who took her with several other girls into the small, white tile room while they sat in desks with little trays like kindergarteners.

"She asked us if we knew what we were doing and if we agreed to it. I told her no. I wanted to keep my baby. I cried so hard, she jerked my arm and took me out of the room," she said, crying openly now. Her brother looked up curiously at her, but with a shrug of his innocent shoulders, returned to play. The clank of the iron chains of the children's swings intermingled with the children's laughter as the park began to fill up with kids, bored babysitters and unobservant mothers.

"My mom came and walked with me into the examination room. At least I thought that is what it was," she recalled, collecting her breath. "But the next thing I know, a nurse came in with a pill she told me was an antibiotic. But that wasn't any antibiotic.

"All I heard while I slept was what sounded like a vacuum cleaner stuck on top of a bucket of water. Then I woke up in my bedroom at home, and it was all over" She fell into my arms, and her entire body shook with her sobs.

"I'll never forgive myself for killing my baby!"

I held her while she cried, feeling her body crack open and

misery pour out like the sand from the bucket KitKat was holding over her head. I didn't know what to say so I didn't say anything at all for a minute or two.

"Samantha, listen to me," I finally croaked over the lump in my throat. "You are not responsible for this abortion. That was your parent's decision. You must, however, take responsibility for getting yourself in this position, but you must forgive yourself as well. We all make mistakes. You know in your heart that if the choice had been yours to make, you would have chosen differently and kept your baby. Find your peace in that.

"Your parents did what they thought was best for you. I'm not saying you've got to agree with them or even forget this happened. But I am saying if you truly wanted that baby then commit yourself to creating a wonderful life for yourself in honor of that baby. And when you get older, you will meet the right man because you are wiser for this happening, and the babies you will have with him will be lucky to have you as a mother."

Those words reverberated in my mind over and over as I related them to my own mother's situation. What must it feel like to be pampered and spoiled by your parents, only to have them turn against you in your most dire life need? And turn you away from what obviously was the love of your life because of social dynamics? I did the mental math and realized she must have met my father shortly thereafter and married him right after her father died of a heart attack the following year. I met my maternal grandmother at my mother's funeral for the first time and never saw her again.

The slam of the screen door to my left woke me from my reverie as Samuel bounded out, a picnic basket on his arm and bellowing, "I'm so sorry. I had to take a call about a child abuse case I'm overseeing in Gwinnett County. I grabbed some of

Mavis' chicken salad sandwiches, chips and some other goodies I threw in when she wasn't looking. I even conned her into cutting one of her pecan pies she's serving for supper. Boy, I hope you didn't have plans for today, because I've got a full day planned."

Because he looked so happy. Because the lines of sorrow I had seen wrinkling the corners of his eyes were fading. Because the back of his hair was still wet and curled over his collar in almost ringlets. Because it had been forever, if ever, that anyone actually planned a day with me in mind, I took his outstretched hand with no questions asked and practically skipped like a little girl beside him to his waiting car.

Chapter 13

I guess car was too simple a term to apply as I lowered myself into the arms of a royal blue Viper Cuda convertible with the top down. Samuel didn't bother opening his door as he swung his long legs over and roared the engine to life.

"Like it?" He asked rhetorically as he could see the awe in my face. "My father bought this in 1973 and treated it like his fourth child. He even had a custom built garage off our home outside of Atlanta, and we were guaranteed decapitation if we dared even look too hard in that direction."

I didn't know much about cars, but the white walls of the tires reflecting in the spotless chrome rims spoke volumes of its importance.

"Did you steal it when you ran away from home?" I asked loving the way the wind blew out my still wet hair. I undid the clasp I had thrown on earlier before we took off in order to get the full effect of freedom that a convertible inevitably provides.

"Just about. My two older brothers still hold a grudge against me for snagging this one. Although they got their cute little foreign hotties when they graduated high school, both of them spit fire when Dad told them he was giving the baby the keys when I graduated law school.

"Sarah always said she married me for this car. She would take it on weekends I worked, which was just about every one, and go riding in the North Georgia Mountains. In one of my weaker moments this past year, I almost gave it back to my Dad. Now that things are a little easier, I'm glad I still have it with me. It sure manages well in rush hour traffic in downtown Atlanta!"

I smiled with him at his memories. "Not that it really matters as I am on vacation with absolutely no agenda whatsoever. But I am curious as to what you exactly have in mind for the day, Uncle Samuel," I said, holding my blowing hair off my forehead and looking to my left.

Samuel was wearing a white t-shirt with a designer's name, expensive I might add, blazoned across the front in navy. I had already deduced before I even saw his car that he probably had money, now I realized he not only had it, but also came from it. The shirt matched his navy shorts that hung down his thighs and again, he sported his Birkenstock sandals. He wore wrap-around Oakley sunglasses that I could only assume were prescription as there was no sign of his glasses. I felt comfortable and relaxed and let my hair fly once again around my face.

"You'll see," he said mysteriously. "Don't worry, your virtue is safe with me. But we're going to attack this day as two people we want to be rather than the two people we have been. We're going to laugh, joke, spend money, eat too much and then come back to the scandalous gossip of our church-loving friends that maybe we started a sordid affair!"

"Whew, all in one day?" I said, laughing. "I'm glad I took a bath." And we took a left onto Highway 231, our backs to the fast food restaurants and gas stations that congregate around interstates and raced the ten miles to the quaint town of Sunset Hills.

Sunset Hills held stubbornly to its minimalist nature and allowed surrounding communities to prostitute themselves with the lure of big money water parks, high-rise condominiums and airbrush enterprises. Ranch-style homes with palm trees, crepe myrtles and wild foliage dotted the highway leading into town with flags welcoming you from their doorways to announce the season, the sport or the holy spirit. The town limits consisted, of course, of Main Street, with three four-way stops that circumnavigated the traditional town square at its epicenter.

We slowed to the requested twenty-five mph as the highway narrowed into Main Street and aging oaks blanketed the sky and almost blocked the sun from our view overhead. There were no cars in sight and pedestrian traffic consisted mainly of children riding scooters, a stray dog trotting across the street with his tongue wagging in time with his tail and an overweight lady with bright red coiffed hair sweeping a store front that read "Curls and Twirls." The only sound was a crackly James Taylor gently crooning on the singular radio station about fire and rain.

Samuel turned into the first strip of shops on the right with low-slung tin roofs anchored by the hair salon and turned to me in excitement.

"First things first. I am going to introduce you to the joys and antioxidants of fresh brewed tea."

"Here?" I asked incredulously. The concrete steps in front of the convertible walked up to a covered sidewalk where the change in awning signified the changing enterprise on Main Street.

"Right here, my friend. Welcome to Biscuits and Business. There's no sign, but I got lucky when I had to resort to purchasing instant green tea at the Stop and Shop," he said with a grimace. "But the cashier told me they didn't sell that hoo doo stuff there. He then directed me to the new love of my life, Mrs. Madeline James, proprietor of the fine establishment you see in front of you."

As I unfolded myself out of the convertible with my rear still vibrating from riding so low to the ground, I glanced at the set of shops in front of me. Just to the left of "Curls and Twirls", which on closer examination was a clothing store as well as beauty parlor, was a glassed-in storefront with a small sign to the right of the pull-to door that read:

Biscuits and Business

We've Got the Biscuits; We Need Your Business

Catchy, I thought to myself.

"I will be more than happy to accompany you in your need for new-age therapy. But there is no way I am putting any green liquid into my body. I don't care how many diseases it defeats."

Samuel told me he knew I would say that and opened the door for me with a cocky grin. A softly tinkling bell announced our arrival.

The shop was rectangular with red shelves housing hundreds of varieties of tea with tiny paper cups like you test ice cream flavors sitting beside the scoop sitting on our left just inside the door. The shelves hung in sharp contrast to the white walls shadowboxing the black and white linoleum floor that ran the expanse of the room. Delicate parlor tables seating rounds of two to rounds of four scattered before a long bar with about ten swivel stools, every one of them occupied. Long mirrors ran the expanse behind the bar and its opposite wall. A swinging door in the back of the room waved the sweet aroma of brewing tea mingled with fresh dough rising. I could almost picture in my head the two circling in some sort of culinary waltz around my nose and taste buds.

"Samuel, you came back! I thought maybe you'd gone back to HotLanta!" A voice shouted above the clattering dishes and general early morning small town gossip. A short, sprightly woman of about fifty holding a tray of empty coffee cups and crushed white paper napkins materialized out of the crowd like a kernel pops up in the popper. Trashy, was the first thought that came to my mind, which shamed me. The truth was, she wore it well.

She was not a tall woman; maybe about five foot four inches and like most of us carried an extra twenty pounds on her small frame. Her breasts were bound together in a white tank top like two babies in the womb. Buxom blonde came to mind, and her tank top was too low. Her blue-jean mini skirt rode too high, but man if she didn't have the legs to pull it off. I was always envious of anyone vertically challenged like myself that still managed to have legs to her earlobes.

"Madeline, I told you I wasn't going anywhere without a kiss from you," he teased, pulling her to him with a peck on her cheek.

"Honey, I hope you got more will power than I got," she said, pointing a long red fingernail at me. "Whew, that boy just makes me go limp. I tell you what, if I knew Bobby Roy wouldn't spank my bottom, I'd give you a run for your money!"

Before I could correct her misconception about Samuel and me, she left in a whirl of make-up and White Lily perfume.

"Come on. She's harmless. I met Bobby Roy last week, and he puts the good in good ol' boy. She's just a big tease, but knows how to brew some tea."

Samuel then proceeded to educate me on the power of fresh brewed tea and my need to ditch my daily java fix.

Apparently, tea was discovered much like Newton's law of gravity. A Chinese emperor in 2737 BC was waiting for his cup of hygienically boiled water to cool when leaves from an overhead tree fell into the cup. Seeing the liquid turn brown and being of a curious nature, the emperor tasted the tea and found it soothing. Through the centuries, tea evolved by hitching rides with traders and explorers while honing its taste. Ultimately, the maritime refreshment soon became an export all in its own right.

"You can imagine, we didn't always have tea pots," Samuel said. "Around the seventh century, tea was actually formed into bricks. You would break off a chunk and then boil it in water. You would then drink it out of a bowl.

"The teapots we know of today were actually around during that time, but used for wine and water," he added, pulling a terra cotta tea pot from the shelf in front of us, turning it over in his hand like a lover. "Eventually, the pots were used to steep the tea, and you would drink it directly from the spout. Sophistication, appalled at this behavior, demanded the teacup. So, we may all now drink our tea properly today."

"So, I'm assuming this is a little more involved than hanging a little bag of tea in a cup of microwaved water," I said, sniffing the various bowls of tea in front of us.

"My dear, you shame me. So much to teach, so little time," he said, placing a hand over his heart dramatically. I didn't notice when he had replaced his sunglasses with his spectacles, but paired with his wind-blown hair it gave him a nutty professor look.

Samuel went on to describe his preferred method of brewing tea.

"The Gongfu method is by far a more involved process, but with better results. First, you take a porous clay pot such as this one," he described, pulling a pot from the top shelf the color of eggplant. "You fill the pot with hot water to warm it for brewing. Pouring that out, you put about one to two teaspoons of tea into the bottom of the pot and fill it with boiling water. Put the top back on the pot and pour out the water. This will clean the leaves.

"You then add boiling water back to the tea pot and let it brew for a few minutes. While it's brewing, you run the outside of the tea pot under boiling water so that the tea keeps a consistent temperature."

Samuel added that it was equally important to rinse the aroma cups and drinking cups with boiling water as well. I learned you then pour the tea first into the aroma cups and then into the drinking cups.

"Finally, you breathe deeply of the aroma cups before you begin drinking your tea. This allows you the benefit of the multiple sensory delights this fine beverage provides," he said as he filled his paper cup with his selection.

"It's been a long journey to get these folks around here interested in my tea," Madeline returned, wiping her hands on a towel as she walked up behind us. "I had to keep coffee by the gallons and give my tea away until I got them converted. It sure is nice to be around folks that know what they're talking about."

"Well, my love, we have on our hands a virgin. A gentle flower in need of nurture and love," Samuel said, looking at Madeline from behind me with both hands on my shoulders. "My friend Melanie has never tasted from the sweet nectar of fresh brewed tea."

"Well, Lord, honey. Why didn't you just say so? Samuel, you just grab you two some biscuits off the counter, and I will be right back," she said, flying over the tea shelf in a flurry of accumulating her potions and returned to the kitchen in a flash.

"You heard the lady. Come on; sit with me in the corner. I promise you won't be disappointed."

We found an empty table by the front window and for a minute just watched the lazy crawl of a small town coming to life.

Across the street was the First Community Bank with a Baptist Church on its right arm. Green space was not an issue for this town as sitting parks interrupted brick, and Main Street meandered around the town square, which you could just see down the road. Tall light posts held baskets of begonia and lantana, but the majority of the town seemed to be settled in at the Biscuits and Business. There wasn't the first fast food joint, and the only gas station was a beat-up Chevron where I would imagine a ten-minute oil change was as foreign to its proprietor as a radar gun was to the local police. It was completely unnecessary.

Madeline returned in about ten minutes holding a steaming pot of the sweetest smell I had ever known. She placed two cups each in front of us and placed the pot on a trivet in the center of the table beside the bud vase holding a single daisy.

"Be gentle with her, Samuel. You know how overwhelming the first time can be," she said, giving me a wink. She turned to a rather large, red-faced man wearing a grease-spotted mechanics shirt sitting at the bar and said, "Come on, Earl. I've never known you to be on no diet. Eat you a couple more biscuits."

Dutifully, Samuel took the teapot and poured it gently into what I assume was my aroma cup. Following my earlier instructions, I inhaled the most delicious blend of cinnamon and rose and continued breathing with my eyes closed.

"Honey, that's only half the joy. Don't waste all your time on foreplay. Now it's time to take the plunge," Samuel said.

I followed his example and transferred the tea to a second cup on my left. I sweetened the mixture by putting a few dollops of honey that sat beside the cream and sugar into my cup and then slowly lifted the drinking cup to my lips. I blew gently on the yellow colored liquid, careful not to spill, and sipped. To the delight of my tongue, the smell was merely the opening act of the symphony of tastes that entered my mouth. I leaned back and sighed in contentment.

When I opened my eyes, I noticed Samuel watching me with an amused expression.

"Feeling pretty proud of yourself, aren't you?" I asked.

"I have to say I am. You are now in the throes of the effect of green tea brewed properly. You'll never go back to coffee again. It's like cheating on your spouse with a two-bit whore," he said, sipping his own tea.

We declined the biscuits Madeline offered and were surprised when she said the tea was on the house.

"We should never cheapen your first time with money," she said with a laugh. She put her tray on the table beside us and pulled up a chair, uninvited I might add, but more than welcome.

"Let me tell you how some redneck Florida gal like myself got hooked on this love," she said, settling in for a story.

Chapter 14

Madeline proved quite the storyteller as we sat enthralled with her recount of the English nomad that crossed the Sunset Hills borders some twenty years ago.

"He was every bit of eighteen years old, barely legal if you know what I mean," she said, giving us a wink and a view of her ample breasts. "He was coming up from Florida having flown across the pond into Miami and wanted to see the states as he called them." Her golden loop earrings swung heavily under the folds of her bottle blonde hair, and she absently pulled a stray strand behind her ear.

Samuel never took his eyes off her breasts. There is just something Freudian about men and a woman's chest. I can't say I blamed him, though, as I was rather hypnotized by the unencumbered swaying. The café had slowed down by this point, and we shared the room with an elderly couple two tables up.

"That boy was something, let me tell you. I hadn't married Bobby Roy yet, cause I was something of a late bloomer. I worked here with my grandma who started making biscuits before Jesus hammered his first nail. Colin came bounding in here one winter day and rocked my world," she said, completely lost in her memories.

Apparently, what Colin lacked in age he made up for in creativity, and he and Madeline spent many a passionate afternoon wrapped up in the moment, in the tide of the ocean and in each other.

"Why didn't he stay? Or why didn't you go?" I asked curiously. I was a hopeless romantic that lived vicariously through other's stories of passion and drama. My life was like a basketball being passed from the domineering arms of my mother to the emotional absence of my father to the capable hands of my husband. I yearned for the kick you in the gut kind of love I always read about in my books.

"Oh, we knew from the beginning he was never going to stay," she said, matter of fact. "And there was nowhere for me to go. He made it straight out that he was going to see the states. But while he was here, we loved so much and so deep. He was the one that taught me and Grandma about drinking tea, and I've been hooked ever since."

"Did you ever know what happened to him?" Samuel asked, seemingly as enthralled as I was by the story.

"No. Shortly after he left, I saw Bobby Roy again. We had gone to high school together, but he joined the army, married some Korean woman, but divorced her before he ever made port in California. He sent her on back home, and then he came on home to me. We've been married going on twenty years, and Samuel here is the first one that's ever tempted me since then," she said, patting Samuel on the hand and lifting up from the table. "I got to get to work now, cleaning up from these messy varmints. Next time you come to Sunset Hills, you come see old Madeline, you here?"

"It will be the first place I come," I promised her faithfully.

As we made our way out of the restaurant, I glanced to my left at the Curls and Twirls.

"Hold on one minute, Samuel," I said grabbing his arm as he

started down the steps toward the car. "I won't be but a second."

The last twenty-four hours had been such an eye opener for me, and I had to admit grudgingly to myself that it was exactly what Rob was hoping I would accomplish. It was as if I took the splintered glass of my life and carefully recreated the window of clarity. I could have bought a second home in Sunset Hills with all the money I spent on therapists and self-help books when the knowledge of what I really needed began inching its way into my consciousness. I glanced back over my shoulder at the man who had guided me on this journey and opened the door.

Ten minutes later I emerged wearing a sleeveless black shirt that read "Florida or Bust" and a blue jean mini skirt with thick-soled flip-flops. I was grinning from ear to ear and struck a pose with one hand on my hip and the other in the air like I was a Barker girl on the Price is Right. If only the PTA board could see me now! Samuel whistled wolfishly from behind the wheel of his car.

"Look at you! You look like you belong in high school. Not riding around with some old fart like me," he said, growling like a tiger on the prowl. "You better get in this car before Earl down at the Chevron looks up from under that hood he's working on."

I laughed in appreciation and climbed into the passenger side.

"I don't know what's gotten into me. I just feel like I need to embrace my trashy side. I grew up with a mother who wore this type of clothing to church, and it always embarrassed me. I promised myself I would never belittle myself like she did. But I'm beginning to think there may be something to loosening up a little bit. What do you think?"

"I think you wear it well," he said starting the engine and

carefully backing out onto Main Street. "I knew underneath that buttoned-up shirt lay some fire. You're right, though. I had not heard that story from Madeline this week about her English fling, but it teaches you to embrace what you have and not demean it by forcing it to be something it isn't. I guess the old Latin term Carpe Diem applies. So, let's get to it!"

He drove a couple of blocks and turned left onto a dusty road that plunged right into the mouth of the ocean. He pulled into the public parking lot and turned off the ignition.

His arm brushed against my bare legs as he reached across my lap to open the glove compartment. I felt a shiver in my lower stomach and a thrill at his touch. Silly, I thought to myself, but nonetheless shifted in my seat to minimize the contact.

Samuel withdrew two kites from the glove compartment and extended one to me.

"Let's go be kids," he said and bounded out of the car like a three year old with his first ice cream.

The day was growing hotter, but the ocean was always dependable to provide a breeze no matter the season. Sunset Hills rested on the Atlantic Ocean, miles away from the sugar white beaches of the Gulf of which I was accustomed. The sand on this beach was very grainy and held a mysterious sheen. But the ocean welcomed us with its chorus of waves and undertow with a lone seagull singing in an operatic warm-up. Samuel opened the picnic basket and withdrew a red and white-checkered blanket.

"Allow me," I said and shook out the blanket until it unfolded in the breeze. Laying it on the sand, I put my shoes, the basket, and Samuel's sandals on each corner to prevent it from blowing away. I reached into the basket and was delighted to find a Tupperware container of cheese straws and a bottle of

Chardonnay. Unable to resist, I opened the container and pulled several of the cheddar sticks free.

"I can't believe where the morning has gone," I remarked to Samuel. Looking at my watch I realized it was already close to noon. "I might want to act like a kid, but my body still screams that I'm twenty-one." I looked up at him with the sun on the shoulders of his t-shirt and waited for him to catch the joke. He didn't disappoint me.

"Yeah, if you're twenty-one then I'm still in high school. But you're right; I'm starving, too. Let's have lunch before we play."

He spread the chicken salad sandwiches and potato salad onto the blanket and lowered himself to lay parallel on his right side, the top of his head toward the ocean. Sitting up on his right elbow, he popped a few cheese straws in his mouth while I uncorked the wine and poured it into the wine glasses with SP etched into the crystal.

Samuel shared with me some tales of courtroom drama and broke my heart with the stories of neglect and abuse in the children and women he represented the past year.

"There was this one woman, absolutely beautiful. She had long blonde hair, about the length of yours, with big brown eyes, perfect skin. Perfect if you could overlook the yellowing bruises like fingerprints on her upper arms," he said in disgust. "Come to find out, she had been sexually abused as a child by her ultra-religious father. He was a deacon by day, but the devil at night. Luckily, there was never penetration, but he would play sex games with her. It wasn't until she was older that she even realized this was wrong. He was dead by then so she had no way to ever reconcile that violation.

"She then married someone she thought was the antithesis of her father. And in many ways he was. He had priors a mile long, starting as a juvie. But it wasn't hard to convince her that she forced him to hit her. That it was her fault he broke her arm when he slung her into the wall. All he asked was for her to get him a beer, not give him any back talk."

"What happened to her? Did you get him put away?" I asked.

He looked up toward the sky for so long I didn't think he was going to answer. Finally, he looked back at me and said sadly, "No, she wouldn't press charges. We couldn't force her to testify against him because they were still married. So, even if the state charged him with spousal abuse, without her testimony, there was no way we could win. Last I heard he moved them out of state to some job with the railroad. I doubt if she lived out the year."

"Any children?"

"No, thank God. But the sad thing is, she would have made a great mom. She was always baking us stuff, cookies and muffins, whenever she would come talk to our office. But somehow we just couldn't get her to break that vicious cycle. I think the first time he beat her, on their honeymoon I might add, he kicked her repeatedly in her abdomen and ruptured her so badly inside that they had to perform a hysterectomy. That's what I read in the file. She never would talk about it."

I asked him how he could get back up after a let-down like that, and he answered, "Even if you save just one. Just one. That's enough to get you through the ones you lose. I've seen the strongest women face hell in the face only to extinguish the flames with one spit back. Those are the ones you continue fighting for. They are stronger than I'll ever be. So, it's not me that's the hero in all this. It's the ones that turn their backs on years of abuse for new lives with worth and value.

"Enough about me. What did you want to be when you

didn't have children?" He asked, the wind blowing his hair around his face as he lay on his side and returned his attention to me.

"I don't remember a time I didn't have kids. It seems I walked into my house sixteen years ago and just now found the front door again," I replied, only halfway joking. "But I thought I wanted to teach school. There was just something noble about forming young minds."

"What changed your mind?"

"Politics, I guess. Everything in public education is so political that somehow the children get lost. So, I jumped at the chance to stay home with our children instead of droning away for twenty some-odd years just perpetually reaching for that apple of retirement."

"Surely you had other dreams. I mean, I went from professional baseball player to air guitarist for KISS to president of the United States all in about ten years. What else did you want?" He persisted.

"You know what I wanted more than anything to do? When I was in college, I got my first full body massage. It was a gift certificate from the lady whose son I kept while she attended classes. I distinctly remember the smell of that room, jasmine, and candlelight flickering and soft ocean waves on the CD player. I thought to myself, now I would love to learn how to make other people feel this good," I said, sipping my glass of wine as my eyes closed to the memory.

"You should do it, Melanie," he encouraged. "Why wouldn't you?"

"I don't know. I guess there is always something lower class about providing that kind of service. Like it's a front for sexual favors. A high dollar prostitution ring if you will. Anyway, who knows? I just might do it one day," I declared more to myself than to Samuel. It was so easy to relax in his company.

We talked some more about Sunset Hills, and I questioned how it was that it had remained such a small town with so much beachfront property. I had lived with Rob long enough to spot prime real estate, and it amazed me there were no sell-outs here.

"I asked Madeline the same question. She said long ago the founders had enough foresight to write some irretractable ordinances that protected the zoning of the beachfront property. After listening to her repeat some of the verbiage, I realized it sounded pretty ironclad.

"I'm sure eventually the old guard will die out, and the more money hungry of the next generations or so will sell the soul of this community, but at least we get to enjoy it today," he said.

After about an hour of catching up on our lives, Samuel looked up at me lazily and said, "If I don't get up and move around, I'll be forced to take a siesta. Let's go be kids." He grabbed our kites with his right hand, secured my right hand in his left and heaved me up.

We spent the next few hours doing just that. There is just something freeing about doing childish activities. You can't help but laugh and giggle when grown people try to act like kids. In an attempt to get his spider man kite airborne, Samuel ran backward, right over a small child's sandcastle at the edge of the water. I laughed behind my hand at his clumsy attempts to apologize, the young mother's assurances that it was okay and the child's wails to the contrary.

So, we rolled up our proverbial sleeves and worked with the little boy to rebuild his sandcastle until we were sure he was no longer traumatized by the event.

Waving goodbye to our new friend, we collapsed onto our blanket, and he poured me yet another glass of wine. I had long ago quit counting my glasses because Samuel had switched to bottled water, but I could have guessed he would have done that. Instinctively, he knew based on my history with drunk driving that he would need to be the designated driver.

"Tell me more about Miss Essie. You mentioned her last night, but I get the feeling she was pretty important to you. What is your most favorite memory?" He asked.

It didn't take me long to reply as the weekend had brought all repressed memories to life in my mind once again. "I know this isn't my favorite memory, but it is the one that I always remember first when I think of Miss Essie."

Chapter 15

The woods behind our subdivision backed up to a dirt road whose only destination was the hell out of town. It took you to no more homes, no stop and shops, no Fred's department stores, only past the county line towards Mississippi. The only sign of life was a clapboard house with a tin roof and an old black woman rocking her life away on the front porch.

Miss Essie never bothered anybody. I don't even remember her ever leaving her home. I know she didn't have a car. She kept a small vegetable garden in the back with tin plates on broomsticks guarding her produce. I think a local church brought her groceries and ran necessary errands, but I never saw that with my own eyes.

I was about eleven years old that spring and wrestling with the forces inside my body those prepubescent hormones awaken with confusion. I was always in the way of my mama because by that time, she had given up on beauty pageants and had given the full force of her attention to the general male population of our hometown. Daddy stayed at his farm later and later until he gradually became more of an apparition than a physical presence in our home.

I was on spring break and surrounded by the general boredom that comes from being an only child. Margaret was at the beach with her family, and as it is with eleven year olds, it didn't occur to me to have more than one friend. I set out for

Miss Essie's house in the hopes she had some fresh fried pies—apple was my favorite because we picked them right from the tree in her backyard.

The silence of those woods always engulfed me, and although they weren't dense enough to provide any danger, I always hurried through them as if chased by a chainsaw wielding escapee from the state mental hospital.

As I stepped around the final grove of pines guarding the border of the woods, I heard that terrible high-pitched laughter that can only be associated with my worst fear—grade school boys. I knelt down beside the wild foliage and looked frantically around for their presence. My breathing came more rapidly, and I swear you could hear my heart beating as loud as the town-warning siren that screamed across our lazy streets in tornado weather.

I saw Tommy Hillbreth, Jimbo Paxson and another boy I didn't recognize doing some kind of crazy dance in the middle of the road, kicking up dust like they were rock stars with dry ice clouding up around them. Tommy and Jimbo were in my class at school, and Margaret had already professed her undying love for Jimbo. I personally didn't see the attraction because I was still several years away from realizing boys were worth anything more than unscrewing the top off a coke bottle.

It was then I saw Miss Essie's house.

It looked like it was bleeding from open sores as tomatoes were splattered against the wood and ran down into the grass. I saw Tommy pick up another one, and I visibly winced as it thudded against a window. I don't know how it didn't break. I could just make out the outline of Miss Essie's head as it peaked around the window just before the unknown boy reared back and threw another one in her direction.

"Take that, you Cajun coon-ass!" He said, giving the others

high fives for his creativity. This boy had a face that was destined to do time for stealing baby kittens from handicapped nuns. His skin bore the markings of a future in Clearasil that would more than likely scar an otherwise perfectly ugly face.

"Those boys had no reason to do that to Miss Essie," I told Samuel sorrowfully. "They were just mean, flat out mean. I already hated them with all the intensity an eleven year old could just because they were boys. But my hatred knew no limits because of what they did to Miss Essie. But what they did was nothing compared to what I did."

"What did you do?" Samuel asked quietly. The afternoon sun looked like it had birthed teenagers as the beach around us filled up with tanned bodies that wouldn't see cellulite for at least another twenty years.

"Nothing. Absolutely nothing. I sat there and watched those boys torture Miss Essie's house and never said a word about it. Not to my parents. Not to Miss Essie. No one. I don't even know how she got her house cleaned. Probably just let the rain wash it away as if God carefully wiped the house with His tears. Looking back, I think I kept my silence because I was ashamed for anyone to know of my friendship with her," I said thoughtfully.

I reminded Samuel this was the 70s in small-town Alabama. I was already breaking some unwritten code by associating with someone not of my race.

"Miss Essie never said anything to me about it either, but several comments she made over the next few years made me think she knew I was there. One time she said, 'Lawd chile, Miz Melanie, the Lawd gwine take care of those that take care of his chilren, yes He will. Always take care of God's chilren, and the Lawd will take care of you.' I would always get tears in my eyes, and she would wrap me up in her big ol' black arms and kiss the top of my head with forgiveness," I said, trying to imitate her wonderful Cajun dialect.

"Did you ever forgive yourself?" He asked wisely, but continued talking before I could answer. "Wait, before you say anything. Let the lawyer in me give my summation. I think you, like all of us, have made mistakes in your life. And, like all of us, you will make many more. But you are still a good person with a good life. I think you have cloaked yourself in retribution for long enough. How can such little shoulders carry so much of the world's responsibilities?

"It's time to forgive yourself, Melanie. Forgive your Mom. Forgive your Dad. Have you ever just sat back without worrying about who needed to be fed and what homework hadn't been done and just listened to your own heart beat and been grateful?"

While speaking, Samuel rose to his knees and pulled me to mine. As he spoke his last words, he put his hand over my heart and looked so deeply into my eyes I felt the warmth spread to my toes. He then folded me into his arms, and we kneeled there for a minute with him gently rubbing my back. I turned my head to the ocean and just breathed in the scent of him. It was polo cologne; I remembered it well from my teenage years, mixed with salt and just the genuine male scent that seemed to cling to that y chromosome. And for the first time in my life, it was comfortable to just be me.

Pulling back, Samuel reached up to pull the hair from my face and gently kissed me on the lips. There was nothing romantic about the kiss, nothing forward. But a peace flooded my heart and touched my soul so that when he tried to pull away, I held tight for one more minute.

I felt Samuel shift in our embrace and realized he was checking his watch.

"Mel, as much as I hate this, we'd better pack it up. It's almost four o'clock, and I still have something else to show you. We'd better head back."

"Oh, okay," I said shakily and visibly gathered my senses. "But do you think we could stop by a pay phone on the way so I can call my kids?" I asked shocked by the fact this was the first time they had entered my mind the entire afternoon.

"Better than that, let's get our stuff together, and you can use my cell phone on the way back," he volunteered.

In the short amount of time I had known Samuel, it was difficult for me to reconcile the man he described himself to be and the man I had come to know. His sensitivity seemed so natural as to have been a part of him forever. And yet he assured me his metamorphosis came at too high a cost.

"I was married more to my job than to my wife," he had said miserably. "I can't tell you the Saturdays she would want to go for a ride in the mountains, and I kept saying later, honey."

It was the reality of his young wife's death that put a perspective on his life that most people don't get without tragedy. I know I sure never did. The only real tragedy in my life was my mother's death, and that actually brought nothing but relief.

We carefully shook the sand off our blanket and working together, folded it much the same way boy scouts do a flag. We kept catching each other's eyes, and Samuel would give me a lopsided grin with that irresistible dimple. He packed up the few items left for the picnic basket, and I walked ahead to throw away our trash in the can beside the pier.

We climbed into the convertible, and Samuel lifted his hips off the seat in order to retrieve his cell phone from his pocket. Pressing the button to turn it on, he handed it to me.

"Don't forget we're in Florida, so you'll have to dial your

area code with your number," he reminded me. Firing up the engine, he reversed the car out of the parking spot and sped back toward Main Street.

The phone only rang twice before Allie answered, somewhat out of breath.

"Hey, sweet girl. It's Mom. I'm just calling to check on you guys. You okay?" I asked.

"About time, Mom. Guess you're having too much fun to care about us here. Everybody's fine if you can call spending an entire weekend in your room fine. Is this really necessary?" She whined. I could just picture her with her hip against the kitchen counter, biting her cuticles just like I do when I'm aggravated or nervous.

"I think you know the answer to that. Listen, I can't talk long because I'm not on my cell phone. Is your dad around?" I didn't correct Allie like the old me would have done. I didn't get my feelings hurt because she didn't ask how I was doing. I refused to be goaded into an argument because this punishment was of her doing not mine. And I promptly squashed the guilt that was seeping its way into my mind for not being there for her.

"He's cutting the grass. You want me to go get him?"

"No, don't bother him. Just give everybody a kiss for me, and I'll see you tomorrow." It suddenly occurred to me that Allie was just like my mother could have been if she had an ounce of Allie's courage and two parents' unconditional love.

"Hey, Allie? I want you to know I love you for who you are not who I want you to be. I really want us to talk when I get back. Not about the things you've done, but about you as a person. Instead of forcing you to be something you're not, I'd rather you introduce me to the person you are. Think we can do that?" I asked, glancing sideways at Samuel. Never taking his eyes off the road, he gave me a thumbs up in support.

"Mom, have you been drinking?" She asked sarcastically.

"Not enough that I don't know what I'm saying, smart girl. Listen, you just think about how I don't understand you. And I'll think about how you don't understand me. And maybe if we talk to each other about those things, instead of how much of a disappointment we are to each other, maybe we can start learning how to get along a lot better. Worth a shot?" I asked, holding my breath.

"Maaaaybe," she said, drawing out the word in order to give the real me enough time to enter into this conversation. After several seconds of silence, she said with a lighter tone, "Maybe I'll even lend you a CD or two to bring you into this century."

"Let's not go overboard," I said with a laugh. We hung up, and I returned the phone to Samuel with a new glow on my face that had nothing to do with the sunburn on my nose. I reached over and patted him absently on his hand as we flew down the highway back to Serenity Point.

Chapter 16

The kite idea was a little corny even I will admit that. But Melanie seemed to need to loosen up; she was sprung so tight, like she would pop up out of the seat at any moment like a jack in the box. Sarah and I flew kites on our honeymoon, and it was always a guarantee to make a day fun.

The Bahamian beaches that June were picture perfect, and we weren't disappointed our first day more than twelve years ago. Hard to believe we were married almost eleven years when Sarah died. That first day, we packed a cooler with some kites and hit the sugar white sand not yet packed with tourists like us. Sadly, that week was one of the last real vacations we spent together. Sure, we'd fly one weekend for a friend's wedding in Vegas or take in a play at the Fox in Atlanta. But never again did we go just for the sake of going. There was always too much work to do. We'll go next summer, I promise, I would tell her. Same excuse I would give for having children.

"It's just not the right time. Let's wait until things lighten up a little," I would plead, not really convinced as I was saying the words that things ever would. And they didn't. And then it was too late.

Watching Melanie talk to the little boy whose sand castle I destroyed put a lump in my throat making it hard to breathe. I couldn't believe what I missed with Sarah by my own stupid choices and priorities.

I shared these feelings with Melanie.

"Sarah always wanted children. She was already a mother to her class, so nurturing and good to them and for them. She purposefully taught in a lower economic section of the city even though it meant a longer commute for her. She felt she had more to offer to children who needed so much," I explained as we lounged on the blanket. Melanie was sipping her wine as I opened a bottle of water. Given what I had learned about her mother, I tempered my alcohol intake to sobriety level.

"She sounds amazing. I hate to hear you blaming yourself for things you feel Sarah didn't get a chance to experience. Unless you purposefully killed her, you had no way of knowing her destiny. Maybe her destiny was to touch your life and those around her, and she fulfilled it much quicker than most of us do in our lifetimes."

I considered that for a moment. "I always like to think that God just couldn't stand to be away from her anymore. She was so wonderful that He took her earlier than expected to teach His child angels in Heaven. That is the only thing that makes sense to me so I sort of hang on to that."

"I think that is absolutely beautiful. What a wonderful way to put it."

As she was speaking, I was trying to compare the Melanie of today with the Melanie of yesterday. Not much change in the sense of her uncanny perception of me and how easy it was to talk to her. But her smile truly lit up her face today, her eyes seemed to be alive with a sparkle of amusement or sadness or whatever emotion the conversation demanded. She looked adventurous in her tank top and miniskirt. And even on more than one occasion I had to avert my eyes when she neglected to keep her knees together when changing positions.

I wondered if I was beginning to change as well. I felt like I was slowly emerging from a dark abyss. Before, I saved my concern and compassion for my clients. At the close of the day, I sheltered myself from the emotions of the world by simply going home to my townhouse, which looked exactly like it did the night Sarah died. Right down to her toothbrush with a glob of toothpaste between its bristles because she was always late for work and never cleaned it. Her Jeep still rested in our driveway with the gas gauge slightly above empty.

Watching Melanie struggle through her own admissions, some I venture she had yet to share with me, made me ashamed at how cowardly I had affected my change.

"Hello, Samuel, are you in there?" She asked me, waving her hand in front of my face to interrupt my revelry.

"I'm sorry. I was just looking at you and thinking how fun you look in your cheesy t-shirt and skirt. It made me realize that I had a metamorphosis of my own to experience."

"What do you mean?"

"I was just thinking that how can someone change if they always do what they've always done? I mean, how can I expect to begin to live again when my entire life is exactly as it was when Sarah was alive? This may sound crazy, but there is still a pile of her laundry on the washing machine, because I keep thinking that if I don't wash it, she eventually will return to do that. Her towel she used last is still behind our bathroom door. How can I expect to move on if I still park beside her Jeep every day when I return home from work? Pretty pathetic, huh?"

"I think it is beautiful. I can't imagine someone loving me that much. Maybe you just needed time to get your strength back. To realize it isn't disloyal to feel what you are just now beginning to feel. And to realize Sarah would love you even more for not giving up on yourself.

"Rob and I have been together a long time. I know this

doesn't sound very modern age, but he is the only man I've ever known. But even with all that history, I can't imagine if I wasn't here that Rob would be all that affected except for logistically. I thought about that last night. Have we been together so long that we have grown out of love and into sort of a comfortable numbness? Have we become, I don't know, like old wallpaper that no one even notices anymore when they walk into the room?" She had sat up by this time; legs curled up beside her, and retrieved a grape from the paper bag. She asked this with a hint of sadness.

She had talked very little of her children, less about her husband. It was almost as if it were painful to discuss either. I guess that was what Miss Mavis meant by her suffering from life letting her down rather than a loss of life itself. But the pain was evident in her eyes when she spoke now, and it was everything I could do not to hunt her husband down and share the gut wrenching world of living with the guilt of not appreciating the one you love the most until it is too late.

Chapter 17

I distinctly remember the first time Rob kissed me. I'm not talking about the chaste peck on the cheek following our first date to Mr. G's Pizza or the exploratory touch of our tongues after the homecoming dance. It was one Saturday afternoon when we were lounging around my den—Rob never wanted to go to his house although I craved the instant combustion that followed any door opening to his cramped family of five. He was always escaping the noise and ability to get lost in the crowd whereas I found it fascinating. Like looking at a foreign land in my history books at school and imagining what it would be like to visit.

But Rob was the son my father never had, and Rob basked in the undivided attention. There was a sense of relief when Rob entered my life for I was able to share the responsibility of my father's love. Luckily on this day, Dad was at the farm, and I had pouted enough that Rob stayed home with me.

He started his tickle game. I always knew it was his immature and clumsy way of touching my breasts by pretending to tickle my ribs. Back then it just thrilled me that he loved me. ME! And I knew he did. There was never a doubt in my mind then or any other time through the years that Rob loved me. I just never understood why. And I certainly never trusted it having never experienced it. But his love always pulled me back from the clutches of my downward spirals. He never understood where I went during those dark moments, but he was always waiting for me when I returned.

After the five-minute torture session, I lay on my back, my hair flying wildly around my face. Unlike most of my counterparts in the 80s, I didn't wear much makeup and was very conservative in my dress. That day I was wearing gray sweat pants and Rob's football jersey with bare feet. I can't even remember what Rob was wearing although it was probably his customary Led Zeppelin t-shirt and jeans.

He leaned up on his side, keeping one hand on my stomach under my shirt. The look on his face was so serious, like he was a sheriff sent to deliver a death notice. He had buzzed his auburn hair along with the rest of the football team due to their win at Regionals so his face was unencumbered as he leaned toward my face.

Suddenly, the world went black, and I swam deliciously around a pool of desire that I never wanted to surface. Rob turned his face just as his nose was about to touch mine and absolutely devoured my mouth like it was steak to a starving man. And I feasted right back. His tongue swept across mine sending waves down my stomach and into places I had not even touched in any kind of intimate way before. He rolled his body on top of mine, and they fit together perfectly.

I instinctively placed my hands on his hips as he raced his fingers up both sides of my head, making fists in my hair as our bodies began to move together. I discovered desire that day, but I also discovered power in creating desire. Strangely, it was more powerful to create desire in Rob than it was to create love. I had no idea what to do with it. Still don't to this day.

But we loved with our tongues and our hands through our clothes for another year before we consummated our relationship. We had actually just graduated high school and had been accepted to the state university. It was early summer, and I was closing up the pool at dusk. You could hear the final golf carts hum their way up the eighteenth hole, which was situated just behind the pool and the clink of the chain-linked fence as the Johnson kids took their bikes off the rack and pedaled home.

"You want me to put the ropes up, baby girl?" Rob asked from the deep end as I emptied the drains in the far end of the shallow. The pool curved around at a right angle with the lifeguard stand at its axis beside the slide in the middle of the shallow and deep ends.

"Please. I'll be back there in a second," I answered walking back around to the lifeguard stand where I grabbed the ring and shepherd's hook, which luckily I never used in all three years as a lifeguard.

The closest I came was the summer before. Sally Hanson had just relieved me from my shift, and I went into the equipment room to retrieve the kit used to test the chemical levels of the pool. Before I returned, I heard what sounded like someone had just hit a watermelon with a baseball bat. I ran outside to find four-year-old Trey Watson unconscious on the concrete by the high dive. I pieced together over the next few minutes that he had slipped off the top step and did a half turn in the air to land on his right ear.

Luckily, Dr. Snyder was on the eighteenth hole and came running when hearing the commotion. Sally and Dr. Snyder administered first aid to Trey while I called 911. Trey suffered a concussion, and we instituted an age minimum on the high dive going forward.

I walked into the shower room, which also served as the equipment room when Rob jumped out from around the corner. It was dark by this time as I didn't bother with the light, and he grabbed me around my waist. Although I wore a one-piece regulation swimsuit, I was still uncomfortable—even at 116 pounds—to walk around without a towel around my waist. Rob was bare-chested in brightly colored jams with water still clinging to his body from his final lap around the pool.

I was always in awe of Rob's raw masculinity. His broad athletic chest narrowed into a tiny waist bound together by ripped abs customary to southern football players. Although he worked hard on his physique, he never put it on display and seemed unaware of its affect on not only me, but also any female within sight. Thank goodness my mother never got a hold of him for he would never have had a chance.

I dropped my equipment as he picked me up and smothered me with kisses. My towel fell to the floor, and I wrapped my legs around his waist like a toddler whose mom was leaving her at daycare. I clung to him while he explored the exposed area of my neck with his tongue.

"Mel, I want you so bad sometimes that I hurt for you," he spoke quietly into my skin. His words tickled the hairs on my ears and sent pulsing waves straight down to my toes. I put my feet back on the ground and turned from him. I walked over to the lockers and grabbed some towels from the bench. I nervously laid the towels across the concrete floor that smelled of soap and sweat, a strangely intoxicating aroma.

Then I boldly slipped my fingers under the straps of my bathing suit and pulled it down to my ankles. Stepping out, I picked it up and threw it at Rob, who I might add had not even taken a breath.

He reached behind himself and turned on the light in the adjacent shower room, which merely bathed me in a distant amber glow. He came up beside me and took me in his arms and kissed me so deeply I thought he would swallow me whole. I never felt him remove his clothes until he pressed himself against me. It was the first time I had fully felt another man's skin on my skin, and we melted into one.

I remember the hard tile of the concrete through the thin beach towels as he laid me down. The concrete rubbed two raw places on my shoulder blades as I moved under Rob's fingers. This was familiar territory for us and not the first time he had worked me into a frenzy with his fingers deep inside me. I felt his hardness press against my hips as I shifted him to a penetrating position.

"Are you sure, baby girl? We've stopped before, I think I can do it again," he said in a voice drowning in air.

I didn't even answer as I bent my knees and pushed up my hips, allowing him full access to my womanhood.

I had heard all about sex from Margaret. She had enjoyed it freely and discriminately with several boyfriends beginning our junior year of high school. But nothing prepared me for the initial shock, the easing of the pain and the pressure that built up within my soul that I thought I would die before Rob released me. I had an orgasm that first night and many more over a lifetime of making love to Rob Graham. Of course, at the time, I had no idea what it was. All I felt was a growing fire working its way out of my inner core and erupting in pulsing waves desperate to find its way out of my body.

I didn't feel particularly guilty about having sex outside marriage. My dad quit going to church after my mom died, but I still maintained an awestruck relationship with God. After all, He was the only one whoever really stuck by me. But deep within me, I knew that Rob would keep me safe forever. And that kind of knowledge had to come from something spiritual. I knew it was the first time for both of us and somehow that made it all right. Although I always spoke of abstinence to Allie and would again to KitKat when the time was right, I knew Rob and I were meant to be together.

Several years into our marriage, Rob brought home a book some of his crew were passing around on a job site about different sexual positions. We also laughed our way through an R rated movie—should have been X—on cable late one night on our fifth wedding anniversary. It was comforting knowing we learned how to please each other with each other and not from other experiences. What we lost out on creativity, we made up for in adventure.

From that day forward, we could never get enough of each other. Margaret took me to my first gynecology appointment and pharmacy to fill my birth control prescription. My Dad found my little pink case while I was packing for college. All he said was, "Well, I'm glad you are being responsible" and quickly walked out of the room.

I never knew why God was so gracious to allow me to be a mother and a wife, but I was determined to succeed perfectly in both endeavors in spite of having no role model for either one.

Rob and I married our sophomore year in college in a small ceremony at the University chapel. There was only family in attendance, and Margaret stood beside me. I was pregnant by my twenty-first birthday. I had Allie at the student infirmary, shivering in the hall with nothing but a cotton blanket to warm my legs that early January morning. Rob was set to graduate in engineering that following winter having taken full loads each summer quarter.

Luckily, I found another young married woman who was as determined as I to finish college so we planned our classes around each other. Not our husbands, but each other. Each quarter, I took night classes, and she would keep her son and my Allie during those five hours each night and vice versa for me during the day. It was a struggle, but a major achievement on my part to receive my diploma only three quarters late. An achievement that went relatively unrecognized by my husband. It led to our first real argument.

I had come home from the frame shop with my diploma and showed it proudly to Rob. There were groceries still in the car; I held the frame in one hand while placing Allie's baby seat onto the kitchen table.

"Looks good," he said in a distracted tone while looking through a drawer. "Say, where did you put the title to my truck? I wanted to go see what kind of deals they have on this year's models."

I walked over to the rickety desk that sat in the corner of our sparse kitchen, yanked open the drawer and practically threw it at him.

"What's wrong with you?" He asked dumbfounded.

"I'll tell you what's wrong with me. I am sitting here with a framed piece of paper that I'm pretty damn proud of. I earned it by going to classes at night all the while washing your clothes, cooking your meals and tending to a newborn baby. And all you can say is looks good?" I exploded on him.

Rob was pretty unprepared for this attack, but over the years grew quite adept at putting me in my place. His primary goal in any argument was to diffuse the situation as quickly as possible so he could move on to the next thing. He liked to say later in our marriage that our fights moved from hysterical to historical. He would joke to our friends that I would win every time because I could remember every little grievance ever committed against me. I didn't find it too funny. The one thing I found most attractive in Rob was the security he provided me. But it was his determination to provide for his family that took him the most away from us.

My life following high school graduation was charmed by most standards. I had somehow escaped the history of tragedy that marked my childhood. My family was healthy; my husband's construction career was successful, which allowed me to focus on the children and their million activities. Life was by all accounts good.

But somehow, soccer games replaced movie nights and passion was replaced by snatches of intimacy in a sort of hurry up before I fall asleep fashion. I learned about romance and addictive love from the library books I checked out weekly. Perspective and priorities went out the window, and life became humdrum for everyone I'm sure, although I was the only one that seemed to want to change that. Sixteen years went by without me even realizing that at some point, no one was even happy anymore, just sort of going through the motions. My perfect family was only perfect from the outside looking in, not looking out.

But like Miss Essie used to say, God takes care of children and fools, and that's how I found myself on that late May afternoon, the setting sun chasing our backs, sitting next to a man I barely knew, but who had made me have that pee-in-your pants kind of laughing day that I had so missed. So, I stood up on my knees and threw an ear splitting "Yee Haw" into the night air in that vintage, gorgeous convertible chariot that sped me on towards the woman I would now become

Chapter 18

We turned right into the dirt road and crunched our way slowly to the guest parking area. My head was resting lazily on the seat, and I was singing softly to Bonnie Rait. When Samuel turned off the ignition, I merely rolled my head towards him with a raised eyebrow as if to say, "What next?"

"Okay, we have two choices. We can either go enjoy an unbelievable dinner by Miss Mavis with all our blue-haired companions. Or we can walk down the road a bit to an absolute dive I discovered on a short trip I took one night. What do you think?" He asked me, hanging his left wrist over the steering wheel and running a finger up the inside of my left arm that hung limply on the seat giving me goose bumps.

"Well, I have to think about this one," I said dreamily, putting a finger on my chin as if pondering the decision. "On one hand, I can walk through those doors up there with no questions asked. A good girl making the right decision so no one will think she has any impure thoughts.

"Or, we can take your short trip in my mini skirt and tank top, kick off my flip flops and pretend for one night that most of the marks on my calendar at home don't consist of soccer practices and book fairs. Gee, that's a tough one, but I think I'll go for the latter," I said without hesitation. My words were flowing together as if in one breath because of the wine that had fused my thoughts into one.

Samuel had told me earlier that in law school in Atlanta, he and friends would escape the madness of 24/7 studies to go on short trips. These trips consisted of no more than a three-hour drive in which the only destination was the blindness and amnesia associated with too much alcohol.

"One time, we drove out to my buddy's hunting cabin outside Newnan," he told me that afternoon. "We drove around in his John Deere ranger with a twelve-gauge and a fifth of Jack Daniels. That was right after midterms, and we were all confident we would never make it to the next semester. So we spent the evening shooting at the tin plates Jack's grandparents used to scare the crows from eating the deer plots. We never bagged a one."

But being the people pleaser that I was, I insisted that we tell Mavis we would not be joining them for supper so she wouldn't go to any trouble. I left Samuel to that task as I snuck upstairs to freshen up. I hurried past the opened door of Mrs. Beecham's room of the New York stage fame.

I could see her in front of her dresser in spandex black tights and a loose fitting white t-shirt with no shoes. She had a black bandanna around her head, and her bare arms were curved in front of her as she squatted in a deep knee-bed in front of the mirror. I couldn't help but watch in amazement as she straightened from her bend, took her left heel in the palm of her left hand and stretched it until her knee locked in position beside her left ear. Her right arm flung out as if she had struck the final pose following a flawless performance on the ice skating rink.

When she lowered her leg, she caught my eye in the corner of her mirror and said with a wink, "That, my dear, is what made a successful fifty-two year marriage."

I bowed gracefully to her in full acknowledgement that I

would require five years of chiropractic care if I even thought about her exercises for too long. Turning in amazement, I walked down the hall to my room, wondering if it wasn't too late to find that kind of flexibility. Maybe that was my problem all along!

Twenty minutes later I crept past the dining room, which was empty except for Nathan who was busily fussing with the place settings. I scooted past the door before he could see me and let myself into the blackness of the front porch devoid of the front porch light. I could not hear the hum of the convertible in the distance and wondered about Samuel.

"No fair, you changed," I admonished him as he stepped out of the darkness by the front walk. He had exchanged his shorts and t-shirt for a faded pair of Levi's, stringy at the bottoms and the pinstriped shirt he was wearing when we met. I glanced down guiltily at my blue jean skirt and tank top and wished I had changed as well.

"I forgot to tell you this about myself," he said mysteriously as we walked towards the beach. "I am an absolute klutz. As I was running upstairs to leave my phone on the charger, I snagged my shorts on the door jam and ripped a hole in the pocket. So, I just threw on what was lying on the chair in my room. I did give you a benefit of a big sniff of the underarms first, though. A wipe of deodorant and away I went!"

It was funny because the most I had done was splash cold water on my face and run my toothbrush over my teeth. And really didn't care. I can't remember a time that I ever left my bedroom without lipstick much less ventured outdoors without some color. Although never one to spend a lot of time on myself, I always ensured I was at least put together with a mist of hairspray and swipe of lipstick. But not this weekend. Not today. Maybe not ever again!

"Where exactly are we going? It seems I have spent my entire day asking these questions." The night air surrounded us as the ocean uncurled her fingers to tickle the bottoms of our feet. The air smelled of salt and wind, but the sky was blackened with approaching clouds. It was easy to lose time in the blanket of night, and we walked as if venturing to the ends of the earth with no light to guide our path.

"On my first night here, last Wednesday evening around five-thirty, I came out on the beach to do a first glance. You know how you do when you go somewhere unfamiliar. You do a reconnaissance to familiarize yourself before finalizing your point of action. I just sat here gathering my thoughts, losing myself in my memory of Sarah. Trying to hear her voice talk to me. And just off to the right, I began to hear music playing.

"At first, I thought it was someone's radio, but as I looked down the beach, I noticed the next building of any sort was some miles away. I didn't think I could hear the music that clearly from that far away especially with the sound of the ocean. So I took a walk and found Uncle Jesse's place," he said quietly. "Just listen."

So I did. Faintly, I could hear the strings of a banjo holding hands with the stronger blast of a trumpet. Like following the pied piper, we walked blindly toward the sound moving up into the dunes, as a piano joined in the melody. Just around a clump of pampas grass rustling in the wind, I saw an unpainted clapboard house with a naked bulb hanging on the front porch slinging light around as it shook in the wind. The screen door was open, and I went in after an encouraging nudge on my back from Samuel.

I learned later from Uncle Jesse himself that he moved south from Memphis about twenty years ago as the city outgrew his comfort level. He found solace in the simplicity of the ocean and strummed his banjo alone on the beach where he lived until discovered by Mrs. Martha Hughes of Serenity Point one early February morning. After spending some time at the big house helping Mr. Hughes with odds and ends, Mrs. Martha took Uncle Jesse to the old servants quarters walking distance from the main house, and in exchange for occasional entertainment and grounds upkeep, he lived rent free with the only love of his 76-year-old life, his music.

He was a big man whose tan skin was long weathered from his life on the water, about six foot, but with about 270 pounds of stomach stuffed inside a white Hanes undershirt and blue wrangler overalls. His duck boots were untied, and the flaps lay open as if he would kick them off at any moment. Grey wool socks peeked over the tops. His mammoth arms looked like burned sausages, but he embraced his banjo tenderly. He merely nodded us towards the sofa over the film of smoke wafting up from the cigar clenched between his yellowing teeth. His face was wrinkled and worn like a topography map that had been wadded up in someone's long forgotten blue jeans.

To his right was a black baby grand piano, nothing fancy with paint chipping along its hood. Sitting at the helm was a young black boy, about thirteen, whose long fingers flew over the keyboards like my kids with their play stations. He wore a smile that split his face like a crescent moon on a starless night. Sitting at Uncle Jesse's feet was an elderly black man as skinny as Uncle Jesse was fat, his bony knees folded up criss-cross applesauce as Will's kindergarten teacher would say. But his cheeks would blow out as big as a bullfrog when he yelled through his trumpet.

It was a motley crew of musicians as if someone rolled them like dice from a barrel, and this was how they landed. But if you closed your eyes, the vagabonds fused together through music like the tentacles of lightning that were stretching from cloud to cloud outside warning us of the approaching rain. Samuel and I stepped around the small, rectangular coffee table and lowered ourselves into a couch that looked like something I would pass on the side of the road. It was an orange and green weave with stuffing poking out in several places, but strangely comfortable. Like all things about this weekend, it didn't occur to me to feel anything but at home, and I closed my eyes to listen to the music.

They were playing *The Thrill Is Gone*, a tune I fell in love with on a sidewalk café in New Orleans in the early 90s. Rob and I were on the only vacation we had ever taken without the children and decided to visit the Crescent City, as we had never been. The overhead speakers were playing traditional blues when the sweetest voice I ever heard crackled through.

It was BB King who, through my growing love and education of blues music through the years, I would inevitably deem the ambassador of soul. I lapped up the blues as if emerging from a drought into the pouring rain. And tonight, I drank from a fountain poured from the heavens as my new friends cranked out such tunes as *Avalon Blues*, *Candy Man Blues* and the great Muddy Waters tune *Feel Like Going Home*. Samuel just merely glanced to his left at the glow on my face and smiled to himself. Our generation would always be one heartbreak away from truly understanding the blues. But that couldn't stop our longing from afar.

I sang softly to myself along with *Mannish Boy* by Muddy Waters:

I had just hit the *Yeah* long and slow when I suddenly realized they weren't playing anymore, but simply watching me in amusement.

"Mr. Samuel, who have you done brought to my doorstep in all this rain?" Uncle Jesse piped in after the final chords of Muddy Waters faded away. He lumbered himself up from his rickety chair and after stepping over his trumpet player, leaned over the coffee table to take my hand gallantly to his lips.

"You sure are a sight for these sore eyes. I don't think I've seen anything this pretty since I don't know when; especially nobody that knows the blues. What you think, Pricey?" He asked, looking over his shoulder at the piano boy who just giggled.

Suddenly shy, I couldn't find my voice around these gifted musicians. Samuel gave me a chuckle with a knock to the ribs and said, "Well, Uncle Jesse, it looks like the feeling is mutual. Since you've left her speechless, allow me to introduce Melanie Graham, a woman who seems to have rediscovered herself in your music."

Giving him a dirty look over my shoulder, I stood from the couch and said, "Thank you, Uncle Jesse, for allowing me to come in your home. Unlike my friend here, I do have manners and would have preferred a knock before we barged in here unannounced. I hope it is okay."

Uncle Jesse swayed out of the room as if rocking back and forth on broken knees and said over his shoulder, "Samuel knows we don't have any doors on this place. It was given to me by the grace of God. And so I give it back to His children whenever He brings them to these steps. Let me go get something to warm you up."

As if on cue, Pricey jumped up and retrieved several glass tumblers from the bookcase behind him, which obviously served as kitchen cabinets as well. The walls were stripped pine with no pictures or adornment whatsoever. The man sat on a threadbare woven rug on the floor and never moved, only looked up at me shyly from under his bowler hat.

"That's my grandpa," Pricey said, placing a glass in front of Samuel and me. He placed one in the outstretched hand of his grandfather who merely nodded his thanks. "He can't talk. Well, except through his trumpet that is."

While we waited for Uncle Jesse, Pricey told me he was in the seventh grade at the local high school in Sunset Hills. He was hoping to get a music scholarship to the prep school in Tallahassee and then onto the Julliard School of Music in New York City.

"I'm so impressed. I think the most I could think of in the seventh grade was whether to play first base or left field for my middle school softball team," I remarked.

Pricey, whose real name was Jonathan Abrams, was nicknamed Pricey because of his love of clothes. He was wearing a starched white button down, sleeves fastened at his wrists, tucked neatly into a pair of black jeans. He told us he lived with his grandfather because his mother wanted to move to Alabama, but Pricey wanted to remain where he could learn music from his grandfather.

Uncle Jesse lumbered back into the family room carrying a mason jar of clear liquid and reached over to fill our glasses.

"Careful with this, sweet thing. I made it myself," he warned. "Yeah, I found Albert here when I visited the All Saints AME church just off Sanders Street downtown. I was needing the Lord bad, and a good colored church will jolt you down with the spirit quicker than a lightning bolt to the heart. Albert was playing his trumpet, and Pricey was banging away at the piano. Folks were falling all over each other, over the altar and all over the aisles. I knew I found my home then. Only white man in the joint, but no one ever seemed to notice."

Pricey went on to tell us that Albert lost his vocal chords

when he ventured into hostile territory during the Vietnam War, and the ground erupted from what seemed like the fires from hell all around him. It was really the Vietcong launching poisonous gas in the form of grenades, and the smoke seared his esophagus taking his voice with it. His trumpet became his voice, and his music communicated his feelings whether through the joy of gospel or the melancholy melodies of old slave hymns.

I took a sip of my firewater as Jesse called it and immediately lost my breath to the searing flames that raced down my throat. Samuel slapped me repeatedly on my back as I groped wildly around for air. Jesse, Albert and Pricey just laughed at me as the tears streamed down my face.

"I told you to be careful," Jesse hooted, strumming idly on his banjo. "The next sips aren't quite so bad."

And he was right. The liquid grew softer as I bravely tried again, and by the fourth or fifth, my belly grew warm as the storm raged outside as if mad that it wasn't invited to the party.

We spent the evening drinking moonshine and listening to old songs of the South and long forgotten African laments. While blues had its origins across the oceans, it made me think of all the gifted songwriters whose sweet voices never made it from the fields on which they slaved. How many talented musicians were never heard by the white history writers of the Civil War era enough to pull talent from the ignorance of our past and further influence us today?

Somewhere through the evening, Pricey gave me a jar of peanuts and encouraged me to eat. Lucky for me, I did by the fistful, and it was probably my only saving grace. The homebrew had kicked in full force by about ten o'clock, and I had perched on Pricey's piano with no care whatsoever if my legs were properly crossed. Samuel would merely toast me with his glass of poison through the haze of cigar smoke and take a gulp, wipe his mouth with the back of his hand and clumsily push his glasses back up his nose while shaking his head from side to side in tune with the music.

At some point, Pricey and Albert called it a night. As they left, Jesse returned from the kitchen with two steaming cups of black coffee. The bitter taste burned my tongue, but went straight to my head rather than my stomach like the moonshine. He gave me a piece of butter bread, "to soak up the alcohol," he said as he carefully placed his banjo on its stand in the corner like tucking a child into bed.

I hugged Jesse's neck, but my arms merely made it to his shoulders as I stretched over his massive girth. We stood at the screen door and thanked him for the magical evening.

"You are more than welcome, Miss Melanie. I hope you find what it is you are looking for." He looked at me deeply and wisely. "A person should always be comfortable in their own skin. It's all they got to house their spirit."

The storm had settled into a comfortable misty spray as we journeyed back to Serenity Point across the sand. Once again, Samuel took my hand, and I just breathed in the night air of salt and wind. I had my shoes in my right hand and kicked the sand up behind me with each step.

Suddenly, Samuel stopped and put both his hands on my shoulders as he turned me almost roughly to himself. I could make out the lights of Serenity Point over his shoulder. He placed his hands on both sides of my head, caressing my cheeks with both his thumbs.

"I don't really know how to say what I want to say, Melanie. And that is most unusual for me being a lawyer. But I'm more than a little drunk so that gives me courage.

"Speaking of courage, you have given that back to me. I came here in an attempt to find a life again, a new one without Sarah. What you've done is made me realize that I don't have to make a new life. I can just go on with my old life in a new way. I have seen you in the last two days break out of the shell that has kept you encased all these years. I don't know who put you in that shell. Maybe you did more than anyone else," he said tenderly, taking a step closer. "But don't you see how you've chipped your way out? I know I have."

I held my breath as he continued. "I know it seems we should barely know each other, but I feel I've known you forever. Our time together this weekend just being goofy and fun is just what I needed, and I daresay what you needed too. I can't explain the way I feel right now because the way I feel defies logic. But just this weekend I got my breath back. And it doesn't hurt as bad to breathe in and breathe out anymore. What I'm…"

I stopped him by placing my hand over his mouth.

"Samuel, stop. You are giving me credit for things I don't deserve," I said, shaking my head and laying my hand against his cheek. "I don't think any of us truly knows our inner strength, that core foundation that rises up when life demands its attention. Sometimes we don't even hear life screaming at us through the deafness of our own making. But give yourself some credit. You heard the calling—no matter how long it took you. You came here to answer that call and found your way back. In a way, I have too."

He took my hand and placed my palm to his lips. With a gentle kiss, he said, "Well, let's think about this, then. Here's what I want you to do. I want you to go up to your room and consider something. I'm going to go to my car and get a blanket and then come back here to the ocean. I plan to sleep here listening to this wonderful world we get to be a part of in this moment.

"And I'd like for you to join me. But what I want you to clearly understand is that I want you to join me in every way. I can't promise you what tomorrow will bring. Losing Sarah showed me that. But what I do know is that I want to feel your skin on my skin. God, Melanie, for the first time in what seems like forever, I am so desperate to feel alive, to feel life flooding through me," he said in almost anguish, running his right hand through his hair as he turned towards the ocean as if he lost his direction.

"Every time I have touched you this weekend, I have felt alive. God knows this is not the direction I saw us going when I first met you. I don't want to even think about the fact that you're married or about your family or what waits for you back home. Right now I just want your life to pour into mine. I want to go to sleep with your breath against my neck. I want to feel alive with a woman again, to create one pulse out of two and bring two heartbeats together. If we are given tomorrow, we can decide what to do with this then."

By this time, he had turned and walked almost angrily toward the natural path guiding us toward Serenity Point, and I ran to catch up with him. His right arm wrapped tightly around my shoulders, and I felt him shaking as I hugged him close to me around his waist. We were walking beneath a blanket of mist giving our path an almost ethereal quality. I took a deep breath and without saying a word, stopped him, pulled his head down to mine and kissed him deeply and deliciously. I then turned and walked toward the house and never looked back.

It was dark in the house; only the front porch light left on in consideration of us juvenile delinquents as Mavis called us earlier. I snuck up the stairs like a teenager after curfew and let myself into my room. I crossed in front of the bed and let myself into the bathroom, turning on the light and looked into the mirror.

What I saw before me was me, nothing more, nothing less. Just me. I was the me I should have been before I gave myself away—before I gave myself to my husband and my children. And I was happy. I had laughed. I had sung. I had skipped. I had even flown a silly kite. I had drank too much and kissed too often. But I was happy. I sat on the edge of the tub and reflected on all my introductions of the weekend. The two most important people I met did not reside at Serenity Point. Nor was one of them a freckle-faced lawyer from Atlanta. No, the two most important people I met were my mother and myself. I thought I knew us, but I was so wrong.

I stepped over to the tub and sat down on its side. I was not perfect, and my mother was not completely imperfect. Those contradicting terms shook hands in my head and in my heart and melted into the reality of my present. I understood that there were things about myself that I didn't like, but there were more things that I did—same thing about my mother. I didn't have to spend my life hating her for leaving me long before she died or hating myself because I loved her in spite of that. Like me, she was trying to do the best she could do given her set of circumstances. It was just that simple.

After about ten minutes, I lifted myself from the edge of the tub and splashed cold water on my face at the sink. I gave a nod to my disheveled appearance in the mirror and returned to the bedroom. I noticed the slip of paper lying just inside where someone had pushed it under the door. I recognized the handwriting immediately, but I knew in my heart how I would spend my evening before I ever read those beautiful words.

Chapter 19

It was raining the day I married Sarah. Raining on the day I buried her, too. I always associated rain with change, the end of one life and the beginning of another.

"You are the best man I've ever known," I remembered Sarah saying to me on our wedding night. "Never doubt how much I love you. I know there will be times that I will want to walk out. There's no doubt there will be times that you probably will…"

"Hey," I said in protest.

She was still wearing her wedding dress, but had removed her veil. I had loosened the tie on my tux and unbuttoned the top of my shirt as I opened a bottle of champagne. We were staying in the honeymoon suite of the Atlanta Hilton before taking an early flight to the Bahamas. Sarah got up from the customary wing-backed chair on which she was sitting, crossed the room and hooked her hands behind my neck. I leaned in to just breathe in the scent of her.

She giggled. "I'm just kidding. But seriously, what I want you to know is that I will always come back. And I pray that you will always come back. But most importantly, I pray there is never a time when we both want to leave at the same time. I pray there is always someone willing to pull the other one back."

And there always was.

I thought guiltily about my time with Melanie this weekend. I felt guilty because I had rarely thought about Sarah. What does that say about me? What did that say about my professed love for my wife? That within one year, I was already enjoying the company of another woman; someone who was married as well!

It was so dark I could barely see my hand in front of my face. I still had the taste of Melanie's kiss on my mouth, and I ran my tongue over it. I closed my eyes and felt her breasts through her thin t-shirt pressed against my chest and embarrassingly felt myself grow hard as a result.

I walked to my car, stubbornly refusing to listen to the words reality was whispering in my ear. Let me have this one night! I wanted to yell at this voice of reason. Don't I deserve one night? I had lived through a year of hell, and for the first time in forever I felt alive again. Like there was hope for me, yet. Like I didn't die too when I buried Sarah.

"Let me have this!" I screamed inside myself.

I remembered that I didn't have my keys with me, so I turned abruptly back towards the house. I opened the front door carefully and walked along the edges of the foyer towards the staircase in order to avoid the creaking boards. I hurried up the carpeted stairs and noticed that luckily all the lights were off in the rooms upstairs except Melanie's.

Shaking my head against the right thing to do, I opened the door to my room and strode purposefully to my shorts that I had tossed earlier onto the rocker before I changed my mind.

Suddenly, I stopped. I could almost picture Sarah in the room with me. Her head was tilted to one side, that slight smile playing on the corner of her small mouth, her hair falling into her face.

"Forgive me?" I asked her hopefully. I reached out to take her hand, but she vanished under my touch. As I turned, I picked up the pad of paper and pencil from the nightstand, and sat on the bed. I began to write my letter of resignation, resigning from the martyred existence I had known since Sarah's death.

> *Dear Sarah:*
>
> *I need you to know that I will always love you. But I understand now what you knew all along. Death would never separate us. Only not living could ever do that. And so by shutting myself off from love, I have separated our hearts. I hope it is not too late to change that.*
>
> *With your help, I am ready to love again. I've met someone who has shown me how to do that. She's hurting, too. You would have been such a good friend to her. You would have shown her, like you've shown me, that the only real way to live life is by knowing yourself and embracing that reality. Thank you for loving me in spite of my many imperfections. Thank you for being so perfect in yours. Forgive me for not being true to your memory. Be happy that I have found my way back.*
>
> *Knowing how to live yesterday's life once again, I will never be separated from you again.*
>
> *All my love,*
> *Sam*

I tore off the sheet of paper and carefully folded it. Putting it into my pocket, I picked up the pad and began my next letter. But yet this was to the woman who brought me out of my fog. Whose sunshine of a smile lifted the clouds that kept me from remembering what it was like to feel alive. Who reminded me of why I ever fell in love to begin with.

I only hoped my words would not cause her more hurt in her life. I only wanted them to bring her happiness

Chapter 20

I shut the door on my reminiscing of the previous year as I shut the kitchen door with the back of my foot. My time at Serenity Point was so precious to my memory, and the catalyst for all the changes in the last year. My hands were loaded down with a bag of groceries as well as my latest item from the print shop. I practically threw the grocery sack onto the counter, not stopping to pick up the apples as they rolled free of the plastic bag. I couldn't wait to see my business cards.

I pulled the sheets of pale pink card stock paper from the manila folder and held them up to the light like a photographer looking at proofs.

Touche'
The Right Touch at the Right Time
Melanie Graham—Massage Therapist
Call for an In-Home Appointment at 888-534-9090

Oh my gosh, I did it! I hugged the sheet of perforated cards to my chest and twirled around the kitchen. Despite the kids moaning and groaning that I was never home. Despite the fact that everyone now had a list of chores and responsibilities that must be completed each day. Despite my father practically calling me a prostitute. I had achieved my goal.

I took one sheet and carefully pulled a card free. I placed it behind a magnet on the refrigerator and began to put the groceries away. The house was eerily quiet as this was the kids' weekend away. I didn't think I would ever get used to the deafening silence of an empty house. But I had to constantly remind myself it was my decision for them to leave, and I had to find peace with that. But everyone seemed to be okay with the changes, although it took some time. Kit Kat seemed to suffer the most in the beginning because she was so dependent on me. But she gradually grew to enjoy her time away and surprised herself with the new friends she was making.

I glanced up at the clock and was shocked that it read four-thirty. My date was due in an hour so I rushed to my new bathroom and turned on the dual showerheads. The bathroom gleamed in its marble grandeur. I even tiled the walls so it looked like something out of a Roman god's boudoir. But I relished in its tackiness and the floor to ceiling mirror I had installed last week. It was a room in total tribute to the new me, and I basked in its extremeness.

I froze when the doorbell range, my mascara wand halfway to my eyes, mouth agape as we women do when applying eye make-up. I looked at the wrought iron clock hanging on the marble wall and was astounded to see it was only a little after five. He was uncharacteristically early. Closing my short, royal blue satin robe I purchased specifically for this evening, I walked nervously to the front door.

I was nervous because tonight was a night of full circle. I had dated this man for the past year and realized what I had known all along. This man was the love of my life. He was the man I knew I had to spend each moment beside, whether by physical presence or merely in thought. I had finally found the love I had yearned for, the love that gave me goose bumps on my arms and a flutter in my stomach. I guess finally realizing I could make decisions that benefited myself first without my family falling apart allowed me to realize I could also do it beside this man I had loved for what seemed like my entire life.

As I approached the front door, I could see him through the panel windows that encased the frame. He was dressed in navy slacks and a beige button down. He was even holding flowers, although I couldn't tell what kind by the angle he was standing. The fact he was holding flowers at all was a testament to his commitment. I could also see him shifting his weight from side to side, probably in impatience with me for taking so long to answer the door.

I opened the door and threw myself into his arms, wrapping a bare leg around his lower leg and grabbing my flowers. He bent low to kiss me deeply, careful of the flowers behind my back as he returned my embrace, walking me backward into the house and closing the door with his free hand. Leaning back up, he said, "Now, that's a homecoming. I've only been gone a few days, Mel. But I'm not one to complain."

He took me by the shoulders and pulled me away to look at me deeply with those same blue eyes I fell in love with almost twenty-one years ago. "Happy birthday, baby girl. Have I got a night planned for you." I took the hand of my husband, and we walked back into our home.

Rob uncorked a bottle of wine while I returned to the bathroom to finish getting ready. After a quick spray of perfume, I purposefully opened my jewelry drawer and reached far back to retrieve a well-worn piece of paper. I carefully unfolded it and read those hastily scribbled words that first filled my heart with peace almost a year ago tonight.

Melanie,

I am writing this quickly before I change my mind. I don't always do the noble thing, but tonight I must. I don't know if you would have joined me tonight, probably not because I sense your loyalty runs deep. But I'm taking the decision out of your hands. I'm leaving tonight. Hopefully, by the time you read this, I will be gone. I don't have enough willpower to say this to your face so please forgive my cowardice.

Suffice it to say you have brought me back to my life. Now, I've got to go figure out what to do with it. I have no right to make yours harder out of my own selfishness. But one thing I beg of you, please remember this weekend. Take it with you and hopefully give it a permanent place in your heart. Maybe that will give you the courage to be the person you need to be and want to be and deserve to be. You know now where to find that person, Mel. Go get her.

All my love,

Samuel

I never spoke of or to Samuel again. I probably could have. It would have been simple to get his address from Mary Beth the next morning. But there was no need. I had received an email from a friend one time that described people as moving through our lives for a purpose. Some remained for a lifetime, some only for a moment. But each left a marker that changed us forever. That is what Samuel did for me.

Samuel gave me permission to find myself and then be myself. But I had to first dig through the layers of resentment and frustrations that had buried my true identity. I resented my mother for being what I now know is the only way she knew to be. I resented my father for being too weak to save her. But what I realized that in all my resentment of Rob over the years, I was only resenting myself for not being true to myself. For being every bit as weak as those I had unfairly and unjustly deemed so themselves.

When I returned from Serenity Point, I let a week go by while I determined my strategy. Rob was used to my silences, we had built a marriage around them, and so he just spent more time at the farm. Another thing I realized during that week was our marriage was exactly like my parents, without the alcohol. I withdrew from life for a short time, and Rob, not knowing how to bring me back, simply retreated to the security of his farm.

But this time was different. After a week of researching, note taking and careful planning, I gathered the family together in the den on a Friday evening for a discussion that would change our worlds.

Allie and Kit Kat sat together on the leather sofa, while Will lounged at their feet on his stomach. I immediately gave Will a puzzle to work on while we talked because I knew he would never focus on my words unless he had something to do with his hands. Rob sat in his hunter green recliner to the right of the girls, and I stood with my notebook and my back to the television set facing the children like I was giving a summation at a trial.

"I'm sure you've all been wondering what I've been doing this week. I know I haven't been available to you as much as before, but hopefully by the time I'm done, you will all know why."

The only sound was my voice and the clinking of the

wooden puzzle as Will placed the pieces in their appropriate places. Rob looked at me curiously; Allie picked at her fingernails, and Kit Kat just smiled.

"I spent a lot of time while I was gone thinking about the way we run this family. And to be honest with you, there's time for some changes. Big time changes," I said, finally getting their undivided attention. Will even quit playing with the puzzle as I continued. "I realized I do too much for all of you and not enough for myself. That may sound selfish, but it really isn't.

"You see, by doing so much for you, I try to turn you into little me's. And you will grow up having no idea how to be yourself. And what I learned on my trip is that not being yourself is about the worst thing you can be."

"Mom, you're not making any sense," Allie said. "See, I told you she sounded weird on the phone," she said quietly to her sister, nudging her in the side with her elbow.

"Well, let me try to make this clearer."

I spent the next hour describing our life from my perspective. How unfair it was to spend a day cleaning a house only to have them return from school and tear it up again. How unfair it was to spend my evenings and weekends carting everyone to soccer games, baseball games, spend the night parties, and so forth while Dad goes hunting, fishing, or collegiate ball games.

"So, let me describe how things are going to be from now on. In a minute, I am going to pass out a list of responsibilities for each of you. Those lists include dishes, laundry and cleaning your own bathrooms. You will do these things because if you don't, there will be consequences. Your father and I will alternate check point times and decide together the appropriate reward or punishment."

By this time, I was pacing back in front of each of them,

pointing my finger like a drill sergeant and relishing in my new role. I explained to Rob that I had outlined the children's activities and assigned days for each of us to be in charge. If he had a conflict with any activity, it was his responsibility to make other arrangements that did not include me.

And finally, I dropped the bomb. "I am going to begin attending school next month at night. On those three nights a week, you are responsible for your own dinners, bath and homework. And your Dad will be responsible for ensuring you have eaten, bathed and completed your homework."

"What are you going to school to be, Mom? I thought you already were a teacher," Kit Kat asked. It was the first question of the night. Rob still had not said a word.

"Yes, I am Kit Kat. But what I learned was that wasn't what I wanted to do and be the kind of mom I wanted to be. I am going to be a massage therapist. It will allow me to set my own schedule and still allow me to attend your activities and be involved in your schools."

"What's that?" Will asked.

"Sometimes, people have sore backs and shoulders and need someone to rub their soreness out. I will have to attend classes and become certified. But then I will be able to go make people feel better."

"Can you practice on me?" Kit Kat asked hopefully.

"No fair, squirt. I get first dibs. Mom can rub all the stress out of my shoulders from having to deal with you little monsters," Allie added, rubbing her knuckles roughly over her sister's hair. Kit Kat ducked underneath and pushed Allie's arm away with a shove. I hid my chuckle by putting my hand over my mouth while keeping my eyes focused and serious. I didn't want to give up any headway I might have obtained.

As Rob adjusted in his chair, I raised a hand to him and said,

"Rob, I'm sure you have concerns that we can discuss later without the children." He sat back down reluctantly, and I turned my attention back to the children and said, "Now, I will be happy to answer any questions you may have at this time."

There was nothing but silence for what seemed like forever, but what was really just a few seconds. Finally, Allie commented, "Whatever floats your boat mom. But what brought all this on?"

"I'm glad you asked that, Allie. I have decided that I have only one life on this earth, just like we all do. And I don't want to spend another minute of this life unhappy. You guys have brought me more joy than I deserve, but I can't use you as an excuse not to go after the things I want out of my own life. And you should love me enough not to ask me to do that.

"One more thing. Your daddy and I are going to start dating again," I said, grinning over my shoulder at Rob as he raised one eyebrow. "So, every other weekend, we are going to make arrangements for you to go away. Whether that is at a friend's house or at Grandpa's or at Nanny and Poppy Graham's. Regardless of where, your Dad and I will have two weekends a month to get away or just go on a date. Any problem with that?"

"Can I spend the weekend with Max?" Allie asked hopefully.

"Absolutely not. Anymore questions?"

"So many I don't know where to start," Rob said, clearing his throat.

"I'm sure you do. So with that, I will adjourn this meeting after passing out your schedules for next week. You have the weekend to familiarize yourself with them and plan your week accordingly," I said handing each a piece of paper with their name at the top. To their credit, no one said a word and filed out quietly to their rooms.

I walked across the floor to take Rob by the hand. I led him to our room and shut the door behind me. He sank down on the end of the bed, his feet on the floor and looked defeated.

"I didn't know you were so unhappy, Mel. I knew we had problems. I would have to be an idiot not to know that. But how did we let it get this bad? Is our life together that bad?" He asked.

Kneeling down in front of him, I took both his hands in mine and resting them on his legs said, "I don't know, honey. But I know I built my life around you and the kids so much that I lost who I was and what I wanted to be. I found that again, but I also realized I can't be who I've been and be happy anymore. I need you to support me in this.

"And I hate to say it, but I'm going to do it with or without you. I'd rather it be with you, but I'm prepared to move forward even if you stay behind." I held my breath as I waited for his response, scared he would tell me to screw off. That he didn't sign up for this bill of goods when he married me. And he would be right.

Taking his hands and pushing himself off the bed, he knelt down on the floor beside me. His arms hung loosely at his side, and I was shocked when a single tear coursed down his face. I had never seen him cry. After a few seconds of silence, he looked up into my face.

"I can't imagine my life without you. The first time I saw you I knew I wanted to take care of you the rest of our lives. I guess what you're telling me is you no longer need me to take care of you. Where does that leave me?" He asked in a choked voice.

As much as I longed to take him in my arms and tell him never mind just to take away the pain from his face, I resisted. "It leaves us as partners, working out our lives together instead of one figuring it out for the other. I've never experienced that, but I know it is what I want. I know it is what I need. I think we could be pretty good at it, don't you?"

"What if I lose you? I know you'll be successful in anything you set your mind to. What if you find you don't need me anymore?"

That was a question I had asked myself many times this past week. I had reconciled that I could go on without Rob if it meant he could not move forward, as awful and frightening as that would be. So, I wrapped my arms around his neck and said, "Wouldn't it be better that I'm with you because I want to be with you rather than need to be? Somewhere along the way we forgot how much we enjoyed being together, Rob. We used to have so much in common and do so much together. Let's find that again. Let's use our weekends together to refinish furniture the way we used to when we didn't have any money. Let's date in a way we never could when we didn't have any money. And let's spend our money now that we have it on each other by doing things together. Can you make that time for me? Will you let me go fishing with you again?" I asked hopefully. Everything hinged on his reply.

His gentle kiss was his response, and it tasted of salt and water as his tears fell around our mouths, and my tears joined his. We spent the evening in each other's arms, never even leaving the bedroom to tell the kids goodnight. As each banged on our bedroom door for our attention, Rob would yell out, "Go to bed. Your mother and I are wrestling without any clothes on." And they would make the appropriate gagging noises and leave.

I never told Rob about Samuel. Probably should have. But I really needed to keep Samuel to myself. Tucked away and private like my friendship with Miss Essie, all to myself. I don't know if he suspected anything. Rob would rather ignore than confront anyway, so it was just easier to move forward rather than plant any unnecessary seeds of doubt and mistrust.

The next few months were an adjustment for all of us. Just like Rob was scared to give me my independence, I was scared of the way the kids grew in theirs. But I got so busy in my school that I was grateful that they began leaning on each other for advice about school, friends and such. And I also saw Allie mature in the right way this time as she assumed more responsibility in our home. She was just too busy to get in trouble anymore.

Kit Kat made new friends in the neighborhood and now spent afternoons riding bikes up and down the sidewalks rather than right against my side. And Will remained Will—still too wild when left with nothing to do, but learning to channel his energies into more positive things like cleaning his toilet.

And Rob and I fell in love again. But more importantly, I learned to accept and trust his love as something I was worthy of receiving. We remodeled the downstairs together, went to flea markets and to salvage stores to change other people's trash into our treasures. I even began fishing with him on the weekends; learning to love the farm instead of resent it. We rented movies and chased pizza with beer. We got drunk one night and ordered TV Guide's three-volume set of the best duets in country music. Every couple of months we'd crank it up with a bottle of cheap wine and dance naked in the den.

And although he would forget about Will's t-ball practice or Allie's dentist appointment, the world didn't stop turning, and I learned to let them handle it.

And every once in a while, I'd see a cardinal. I learned at some point that seeing a cardinal represented peace in your life. That peace for me came in the form of a lanky limbed lawyer named Samuel Patterson who smiled his way into my heart by leading me to the person I was truly meant to be. And to be that

person with the family who loved me. Samuel found permanent
residence in a small corner of my soul that I had somehow
saved for him my whole life. I just didn't know his name. But
I would always be grateful for him showing me the point of
serenity.

Epilogue

As usual, the return ride home from a vacation never seemed as long as the ride to a vacation. Maybe that was because the anticipation was gone, and the pressures of reality lined the road ahead of you as if watching a parade.

The storm clouds of the past week had long sauntered out to the Atlantic Ocean, and the warm spring air rushed past my face in the convertible. The rain provided a baptism of such, a cleansing to wash away the old and emerge into the new. I purposefully took the long back way home, up the coast through Savannah, preparing to turn the corner to head back to Atlanta and back to my life. And I thought of Melanie.

I was selfish by nature and other than Sarah's death, had more or less always achieved anything I sought. So to know I gave up a night with a woman who stirred things in me long laid dormant surprised even myself. Maybe I gave myself too much credit to think she would have given herself to me anyway. Regardless, I knew the attraction was there for both us; there was no way to deny that.

However, I knew I was not the person to heal her past. Nor was I the man to comfort her present or to provide her future. And she was not the woman to do that for me. But hopefully I introduced her to herself much like I became acquainted with myself. And we both realized we're not so bad and neither is life no matter what it brings us.

I lowered my visor to the rising sun as I drove up the east coast, smiling into the wind as I allowed the two women I have loved so far in my life to rest in peace.

Printed in the United States
64348LVS00002B/67-165

9 781424 159840